THE PISTOL MAN'S
APPRENTICE

Copyright © 2018 by Linell Jeppsen
All rights reserved.

Published in the United States by Wolfpack Publishing

Wolfpack Publishing
6032 Wheat Penny Avenue
Las Vegas, NV 89122

wolfpackpublishing.com

Library of Congress Control Number: 2018951501

Paperback ISBN: 978-1-64119-278-1
Ebook ISBN: 978-1-64119-277-4

THE PISTOL MAN'S APPRENTICE

LINELL JEPPSEN

WOLFPACK
PUBLISHING
— EST 2013 —

Acknowledgements

I want to thank my editor and friend, Stuart Rosebrook, Ph.D. He spent a great deal of time and energy making sure my time-lines were correct, my political ideas were right, and my train lines and depots were accurate. He caught several mistakes, made numerous suggestions, and did it all with grace and good humor. Without his help (and his daughter Kristina's assistance with the Spanish), this novel would have suffered.

I dedicate this novel to my beloved Danny. For ever and always, he is my hero.

THE PISTOL MAN'S APPRENTICE

Chapter One

_1874_

NINE-YEAR-OLD DANIEL MONROE was about a quarter of a mile away from the wagon train, looking to shoot some rabbits when gunfire shattered the still, muggy air. He immediately crouched as low as he could get—a trick that his father Amos, and his big brother Christian had taught him when they first struck out for Oregon from their home state of Kentucky.

He trembled as more shots rang out. Something was attacking the wagon train and his family. He heard inarticulate shouts, catcalls and laughter as feminine shrieks added to the distant uproar. _Was that Ma?_, he wondered and fought against the urge to stand up and run toward the danger, rather than cower in the dirt like a mouse.

A storm of gunfire pierced Dan's ears and then

silence replaced the thunder, which somehow seemed even more ominous. He lifted himself from the ground and peered through the prairie grass at the semi-circle of wagons in the distance. What he saw made his mouth sag in horror.

It wasn't Injuns, as he'd first feared but a gang of outlaws. They were twenty-strong and had his family and friends surrounded.

There were six wagons in all—four owned or rented by the pilgrims and two owned by the teamsters and their hired cook. There was a small herd of cattle, horses, numerous pigs, and a handful of goats traveling with them. Some of the horses whinnied in fear, broke their hobbles and ran off into the distance, as the men stopped shooting and rounded the travelers up into a tight group.

A few of outlaws rifled through the cook's wagon, grabbing food and stuffing their mouths full while others made their prisoners lie down on the ground. They milled around the group of pilgrims, ransacking their pockets and relieving the men of their firearms.

Dan had good eyesight, but it was hard to make out details with the sun's hot, dusty haze hanging in the air. Still, he thought he saw his mother, and three other women being yanked up off the ground and dragged away to the other side of the low-burning cook fire. He couldn't tell what happened then, but he clearly heard his father Amos, and a few other masculine voices cry out in rage.

Then his brother Christian jumped up from where

he'd been lying on the ground and tried to run after his ma. Dan heard another shot ring out and his big brother fell headfirst into the fire, throwing up a shower of sparks.

Dan could stand it no longer. He hauled himself up off the ground and took off running. He had no idea what he was planning to do but surely, with his rifle, he could help his ma and maybe save his pa, too.

He had run about a hundred yards, when something hit him from behind with a muffled grunt. He squealed in fear, but a big hand covered his nose and mouth, and a harsh, masculine voice hissed in his ear, "Be quiet, kid, or you'll be next!"

He wriggled in the stranger's arms and was then shaken until his teeth clacked together. "You want me to knock you out? I will if you don't stay still and shut up!"

Dan stilled and heard the man's heart thudding against his ear. It was pounding away as fast as his was and he suddenly understood that the man who'd caught him in mid-flight was as scared as he was. That instinctive knowledge won his tentative trust and he fell back against the man's chest.

Looking up he studied his captor's face. He was heavily bearded and quite filthy, but he didn't seem too old... Dan figured he was about his pa's age and Amos was thirty-four-years-old. His hair was dark brown, his beard was streaked with red and gray, and his eyes were green like grass.

He was hunkered low and studying the action

happening by the wagons. His expression was bleak. Then he glanced over at Dan and put one finger over his lips as another volley of shots rang out. Dan felt tears trickle down his cheeks... he knew, abruptly, that his family and friends had just been killed.

The pain he felt at that moment was so huge, so uncontrollable, it was like a big wave crashing over him, drowning his soul in grief. He wanted... no, needed to draw air into his lungs and scream, but the man next to him seemed to sense his intention. The older man grabbed him and pressed his face into his chest—hard.

Dan's howl of sorrow was muffled, but could easily have been heard, if the outlaws weren't making their own racket. They tied their mounts onto the back of the wagons and after seizing anything and everything of value from the camp they drove off, laughing and celebrating a job well done.

After the last wagon disappeared over a rise, the man let Dan go and said, "Come on, kid. We'd better make ourselves scarce."

Dan stared at him—this stranger who was offering companionship and shelter.

Although his face was still wet with tears and his heart felt like a hollow hole in his chest, he understood he was now alone on the Great Plains west of Scotts Bluff—at least 1,000 miles from where his family had hoped to settle.

He had no one to care for him and no means to care for himself. He also had no choice, but he tried to be sensible. Remembering what his ma and pa had told him many times about not trusting strangers, he held out his hand and said, "My... my name's Daniel Monroe. What's yours?"

The man stared down at him with wide, troubled eyes. He looked none too happy with the situation but then he heaved a disgusted sigh, stuck out his hand and said, "Name's Jacob Conrad. Folks call me Jake."

The gunslinger and the little boy shook hands, and then walked a half-mile away to where Jake's gelding and a packhorse were staked out by a tiny creek.

Chapter Two

Jake studied the boy who was sleeping by the cold fire and frowned. *One shot—that's all it would take,* he mused, *and the boy wouldn't even know what hit him. Then, I could beat leather and head north...*

After all—what was one more body added to his kill list? He'd lost count. Still, he hesitated. This kid hadn't done nothing to deserve killing. He was just another unlucky traveler like so many that had come before him... like Jake himself had been so long ago.

He glared at the boy's sleeping body once more, and then got up to feed his two horses a handful of grain from his dwindling stores. The little incident the day before was not only unfortunate for those sorry pilgrims but was messing his plans up something fierce.

He heard a soft sigh and muttered words and walked over to where the boy was waking up. He saw his shadow loom over the kid's face and Dan gasped.

"Wha... NO!" he shouted and tried to grab his little .32 ca. squirrel gun, which was now stowed in one of the packhorse's saddlebags.

"You need to get up now. We're leaving." Jake murmured, and saw the kid rub the sleep and dried tears out of his swollen eyes.

"But, we gotta bury my... my folks," Dan croaked.

Jake sighed, "We ain't burying nothin', kid. That's hardscrabble out there—too hard to dig. We can't burn 'em either, because we're smack dab in the middle of Arapaho, Cheyenne and Sioux country. They see a fire big enough to burn them pilgrims, and they'll come a-running and throw us on top of the pile."

"But..." Dan started to object, but the older man shoved a cup of cold coffee in his face.

"I want you to drink some of this, and then we'll ride on over and see if we can put some rocks over your people, okay? That's the best we can do for them now."

Dan stared into the distance for a moment and took a sip of the cold coffee that was liberally laced with whiskey. He grimaced in disgust and made to throw the rest in the dirt, but Jake barked, "Drink it up, like I told you!"

Shrinking back a little, the boy glared and downed the cup's content in one swallow. It was a fine effort, but Dan sputtered, and gagged. Still, after a few moments, color came back to his cheeks and he seemed steadier.

"You ready to go pick some rocks?" Jake asked.

Dan stood up and said, "Yeah, if that's the best we can do…"

Jake snorted. "It is, kid, believe me."

Dan sighed and walked over to Jake's horse, but the man said, "Go climb on Jonesy. He won't even know you're there."

The big piebald packhorse swiveled its ears and nickered as Dan walked up to him, but seemed friendly enough as he climbed on and perched himself on top of the pack racks. Then he followed Jake out of the shallow ravine and onto the open prairie toward what remained of his family.

Dan could see that Jake was right. He'd not really noticed before, but the ground was packed hard and was mainly gravel and scree. The people in his wagon train were strewn about like fallen cordwood and he wanted to cover his eyes against the horror of it. Still, he searched for and found his pa lying in the middle of a group of dead men.

Amos Monroe's black hair and big, bulky body stood out from the rest, and Dan saw that his pa's cornflower blue eyes were partially open, as if he was observing the sorry scene from someplace far away. Tears pricked at his eyes, but the boy gave them an angry swipe and bent over to see if he could drag his pa away from the other bodies.

"Here, let me give you a hand," Jake was next to him, and his strong, corded wrists seized Amos' ankles and pulled. He dragged Dan's father a distance away by a small, rocky hillside.

Dan watched for a moment and then walked over by the dead cook fire and saw his brother Christian lying half-in, half-out of the stone fire-ring. He'd been shot in the back and his left cheek was burnt down to the bone. Dan heard Jake walk up next to him and saw him bend down to pick Christian up, but Dan protested, "No! Let me do it."

Jake shrugged and stepped away, watching as the much smaller boy picked his older brother up and dragged him slowly toward where his pa lay at rest. Then he glanced over at where the womenfolk lay and gritted his teeth. Jake figured this would be the hardest part for the kid, but Dan walked up and said, "That's my ma—the pretty one in the middle. Can you help me, please? I don't think I can lift her."

The woman Dan pointed to had been very pretty indeed, but death had robbed her of any color and her glossy brown hair lay limp in the dust. Luckily, her rapists had thrown her skirt back over her legs when they were finished with her so her modesty, at least, was spared.

The bullet hole in her forehead was a stark reminder of her violent death, though, and Jake bent down quickly, hoisted the woman in his arms and walked toward the rest of her murdered family as her son followed behind.

The hillock was mainly small rocks and gravel, and although they were unable to do a thorough job without a pick or a shovel, they managed to cover the bodies with enough material so they were hidden from sight and mainly safe from foraging animals.

It was rough work and by the time they were finished the sun was starting to set. Dan stood heaving and covered in dirt and sweat. Then he turned around and started to shake a little at the sight of the other bodies that still awaited burial.

"We... need to..." he stuttered, but Jake shook his head.

"No. It ain't gonna happen. Sorry, but we gotta go."

Dan stared up at him and looked like he was fixing to argue, but he simply nodded and walked toward ole Jonesy on weak-looking legs. Jake had to admire the kid's grit. His palms were bleeding from all his shovel work-done without a shovel, just the edge of a cheap metal pot.

He mounted his horse and watched as the boy climbed up on the packhorse and gazed, one last time, at where his family was buried. Then, Dan clicked his tongue and followed Jake into a whole new life.

Chapter Three
_____

THEY RODE-HARD—FOR TEN DAYS STRAIGHT. THEIR PACE
was so brisk Dan developed blisters on his blisters and
wanted to weep with fatigue. He wanted to complain
to his companion, and gripe about the punishing ride,
but the man had settled into a grim, unfriendly mood.
Dan feared Jake's silence and wondered just what was
going on behind those cool, green eyes.

It felt like they were on the run from something and
more than once, Jake halted their progress and turned
around in his saddle to scope the landscape behind
them. Dan also noticed that the times they *did* stop for
a quick rest or some cold chow that they used the thick
forest and foliage to hide their whereabouts.

He finally screwed up the courage to ask Jake why
they were riding so hard. "Sir, is there someone after
us?" Dan's voice was rusty with disuse, and his words
fell into the silence between them like stones in a
still pond.

Jake frowned and glanced over at him. He stayed still for a moment, but allowed, "Like I told you, this is hostile territory—Arapaho, Cheyenne…" He peered into the distance ahead, adding, "And now, the Sioux."

Dan gazed all around, imagining a hostile Indian behind every tree and shrub. But still, something seemed to be off about the older man's concerns. He thought, *there are Injuns everywhere, how does anyone ever stay alive if the natives are so bad? Unless folks pack together like horses… more strength in numbers.*

"Sir," he ventured, "Maybe we oughta head for a town, you know, other people if the Injuns are so bad?"

But Jake's reaction was a fierce glare and a snarled, "No! No towns where we're going."

The look in Jake's eyes was ugly, and Dan kept his mouth shut for the next two days. They stopped for a cold camp, twice and finally, after a long day following the tree line along a great valley, Jake said, "Watch out, kid. Follow my trail—we're going up from here."

Dan looked to his right and saw an animal trail leading straight up through a forest of aspen and assorted conifers. He tipped his head back and saw the forest stretching as far as his eyes could see.

He sighed. His packhorse was as steady and strong, but Jonesy was footsore from the hard ride and seemed to have developed a left-hoof limp. He would now be required to pick his way through miles of thicket with a heavy load on his back. He screwed up his courage and said, "Jake, sir, I think Jonesy's goin' lame…"

Expecting a harsh reply, Dan was surprised when

Jake turned around with a look of regret. "Dammit! My fault…" He stopped his big gelding and stepped off. "You think you can walk this stretch? It's not that far—maybe two or three miles. Then we can picket these horses and get some rest."

Dan murmured, "Yes, sir," and climbed off the pack-horse. Jake immediately bent over and inspected the horses back hooves, patting Jonesy on the rump. "Sorry, old man. We'll be home soon, alright?"

Dan gazed at his companion with surprise. *This man has a home? And it's right in the middle of Indian territory?*, he wondered… and worried.

Jake interrupted Dan's thoughts. "Okay, we both walk, leading the horses. Like I said, it ain't too far."

Dan tied Jonesy's reins in a loose knot and set out after Jake. The trail was gradual and well traveled. Looking down, he was surprised to see hoof and foot-prints pressed into the soft loam, and thought, *Why, this path is practically a road!* Then, looking closer, he noticed that most of the hoof prints were from unshod horses. *This is an Indian trail!* He thought, prickles of fright tickling the hair on back of his neck.

"Sir…" he whispered.

But Jake turned around with a frown, put his finger over his lips, and said, "Shhh…"

Dan shut his mouth and followed Jake and his horse as silently as possible. They kept walking uphill, and by the time they reached the top of the trail, Dan legs felt like lead and his breath hitched in his chest.

Jake stopped walking, turned around and said, "Stay

here. I'm gonna scout ahead and see if it's clear. It should be, but just in case, take this..." he offered a tarnished, old pocket watch to Dan. "You know how to tell time?"

Dan had been taught once but he'd forgotten the particulars. "Er, not really, sir."

Jake answered, "Don't matter. You see this hand?"

Dan nodded.

"Okay," Jake said, and pointed to the next numeral on the clock's face. "If I'm not back by the time this goes from here—to here, you turn this hoss around and skedaddle oughta here—double-time. Got it?"

"Yessir," Dan answered.

Without another word, Jake mounted up and kicked his horse into a swift walk, quickly disappearing from sight.

Dan stared after Jake for a moment and then glanced around the green, wooded thicket. Now that he was standing still, a million sounds filled the air. The steady swoosh of the tree's tops rubbing together, birdsong, crickets whirring in the shrubbery, the harsh scolding of chipmunks in the high branches, and other scarier noises he couldn't identify.

He was alone for the first time since his family had been murdered, and he didn't like it one bit. What if Jake was sick of him, and tired of sharing his grub with an orphan? What if Jake had gotten sick of his questions, or of tending to his blisters with his own precious liniments? What if...?"

Dan's heart started to pound with fear and he stared

up at the swaying treetops in a near panic. Looking around with wide-eyes, he suddenly spied an unfamiliar figure coming up the trail behind him on silent, moccasined feet.

Dan's thudding heart tripled its beat and he gulped. *An Injun! Coming right at me!*

He wanted to grab his little .32 but it was stowed away on the top of the saddle racks, and the young brave was approaching so swiftly, Dan knew he'd never grab the gun in time to save himself. Not knowing what else to do, Dan stood his ground and held his hand out to shake. "How do you do?" his voice quivered, but he soldiered on. "My name's Daniel Monroe. Pleased to make your acquaintance."

Chapter Four

THE NEWCOMER WAS, APPARENTLY, UNIMPRESSED BY Dan's introduction and passed him by with a glare. Then he grabbed the reins out of Dan's hands and pulled on Jonesy's bridle.

Immediately, the old packhorse pulled right back, and the teenager flew forward and landed on his face in front of the horse's hooves. Dan couldn't help but grin. He had been battling the horse's tendency to stop and nibble at anything and everything edible for the last hundred miles and could have told the Indian what would happen when he grabbed the reins.

He was still scared, though, and didn't want to anger the young man so he covered his smirk with his hand, grabbed a handful of green weeds, and offered it to the other boy as an enticement for Jonesy's greed.

The teenager frowned in disgust for a moment, even as he brushed bark and chaff off his backside. Then he shrugged, held the tasty weeds in front of

Jonesy's nose and led the horse uphill. Dan stayed still for a second and wondered, *Should I follow, or should I turn tail and run while the Injun's not looking?*

Dan studied the boy as he marched up the path, Jonesy in tow. He was probably fifteen or sixteen-years-old, not very tall but lean and fit. His hair was a glossy black and long enough to tie on top of his head in an elaborate, braided bun, which had one cocky feather jutting from it. He wore a pair of leather britches and no shirt. His mocs were decorated with beads and quills, and his woven cloth-belt sported two, long knives.

He looked like a tough customer, and Dan hoped the boy didn't plan on acting out his obvious dislike. As these thoughts swirled around in his head, the boy turned around, said something and waved his arm in a 'come hither' motion. "Well, guess I'm supposed to follow," he murmured, and walked up the path to where the Indian boy and the packhorse had just disappeared.

He walked about 200-yards and stopped, staring at the scene in front of his eyes with amazement. An Indian village was spread out before him. There were about fifteen tipis, two or three large cook fires, tangles of drying racks and an enormous pile of bones and hides right in the middle of everything.

Even as his eyes drank in the sight, he saw several women and children walk over to the pile and grab either a handful of bones or one of the hides. That pile seemed to be a going concern because everything in it was being cooked, cleaned, scraped or gone over in one way or the other.

"They just got in from a good buff hunt," Jake answered Dan's unspoken question.

Dan looked up, startled at the man's sudden, silent appearance and said, "Sir... where are we?"

Jake gazed at the Indian village and seemed to be more relaxed now than Dan had ever seen him. "These are my wife's people. We should be safe here for a while—at least until they move further south for the winter."

Dan's mouth hung open and he stammered, "Sir, you have a wife?"

Jake frowned and shook his head. "Not no more, I don't. But her family still accepts me as family. Like I said, we should be safe here for a while."

Dan wanted to ask why Jake no longer had a wife and what had happened, but Jake's face had settled into that familiar chilly distance, and the boy decided it was best not to pry. Jake stepped forward and said, "Come on, I need to introduce you to my father-in-law."

Dan stepped smart and asked, "What kinda Injuns are these, sir, if you don't mind my asking?"

"These are Northern Cheyenne, Dan. Good friends to have, but not too friendly to most white folks. You be respectful when I introduce you—keep your eyes down and don't sass, okay?"

Dan gawked. "Sir, I would never be sassy!"

Jake grinned. "Yeah I know that. It's just—I don't want to run afoul of these people. They are prideful, and things ain't been going too well for them lately, with all the white settlers and the military moving in."

Dan nodded, "I'll be real respectful, sir, I promise."

Jake glanced down at Dan and thought, *this is a good boy. Pity he's all alone on this earth.*

As they drew closer to the village, Dan heard laughter, dogs barking, children playing and the soft murmur of many older men as they sat watching the white man and boy come closer.

One man stood apart. He was short and stout. Not fat though; his compact body rippled with muscle. His gray hair was plaited into two long braids and he wore feathers and beads on a thong around his neck. His eyes were fierce as he stared down at Dan.

He looked none too friendly and Dan reached up and hooked a finger through Jake's belt. He'd never been this familiar before, but his nerve was failing him. He suddenly pictured himself being lowered into one of the many cook pots scattered throughout the Indian camp.

The teenager who'd led Jonesy up the trail stepped next to the warrior and stood with his arms crossed. He lifted his face to say something to the older man and Dan saw the man bend over to listen. Then the Indian gazed at Jake and Dan as they came to a stop in front of him.

"Welcome home, my son. Who is this white boy you bring to our camp?"

Chapter Five

THEY SPENT TWELVE DAYS AT THE CHEYENNE CAMP. IT was a rocky beginning for Dan who sat in front of the Indian men, enduring harsh questions, which Jake answered, sneers, contemptuous laughter, and finally, watching as the men held their noses and waved their hands in the air as if to ward off an evil odor.

To Dan's utter shame, he realized they were talking about him and how much he stank, and he wanted to die with shame. Before he could, though, a trio of old women walked up to him, seized him by the scruff of the neck like an errant puppy and dumped him, clothes and all, into a cook pot with warm water, and a sliver of Jake's harsh lye soap.

Then, they bent over and started scrubbing the dirt, sweat and grime off his body with rough washrags and a particularly scratchy twig brush. His ears were probed and so was his bottom as the old women set about their task with gusto and humor.

He was, of course, within sight of the rest of the village and it seemed as if everyone, young and old, was enjoying the show. The only thing that soothed his wounded pride was seeing Jake grab a threadbare towel and another small piece of soap out of his saddlebags, and light-out for his own bath.

Finally, the women decided he was clean enough, and let him step out of the pot and dry off. Surprisingly, the teenager who he'd first met walked up to him with a change of clothes—leather britches, and a soft leather tunic. Dan smiled his thanks, and the young man grinned in return.

He stepped into the britches and saw that they fit like a glove, and realized that, despite the humiliating circumstances, he felt better than he had in weeks. The last time he'd looked in a mirror, he'd seen a black-haired, blue-eyed boy who was tall for his age, and sported a happy-go-lucky, gap-toothed grin.

That was weeks and weeks ago, though, and he wondered now if the sorrow of losing his family, and fear of an uncertain future alongside a stranger had changed his countenance any. He'd spent days and days crying himself to sleep during their mad dash away from the wagon train disaster and for most of a week, he'd woken every morning feeling like a hollowed-out gourd.

He looked around and saw one of the women who had dunked him into his mandatory bath gesturing at him with a stiff leather trencher filled with food. His stomach gave out a loud rumble and he realized he was starving. Moving forward, he accepted the stew with a smile of thanks, and sank down on his haunches to eat his first hot meal in over two weeks.

The stew was hot, greasy, slightly sour and one of the best things he'd ever eaten. He used his fingers to pick out the larger chunks of meat and tipped the whole leather slab against his lips to drink down the rest. One of the women said something to him, and although he had no idea what she said, he simply nodded and grinned his enjoyment of the meal.

She laughed at him, grabbed his makeshift plate and filled it with more stew. Dan set—to again and then watched with amazement as Jake walked up and took his own trencher of stew and sat down across from him.

Although he was grateful for Jake's help, Dan had thought the man was kind of a dirty bum. But his transformation was almost unbelievable after a wash-up. His hair was well past his shoulders and looked to be a rusty-blonde color. Jake had shaved his chin-whiskers off, but his mustache was auburn, which highlighted his green eyes and strong, white teeth.

Why, he's a handsome cuss! Dan thought, and understood why Jake had once had a wife. He realized that most women would be proud to call the man, "husband."

"That woman there is my mother-in-law, Dan. Her name is Green Willow Woman," Jake said.

Remembering his manners, Dan stood up and said,

"Hello, Green Willow Woman. My name is Jake. Thanks for the good stew. I loved it."

Jake translated for him and Dan saw the woman cover her smile and nod. She murmured something in reply which he didn't understand, but Jake said, "You are welcome… and you are nice-looking now that you are clean."

Dan blushed but smiled and said, "You clean up good, too, sir."

Jake grinned, but said nothing—he just continued to eat his stew. Finally, he said, "Black Bird will let us sleep in his tipi, and I want you to go there now and get some shut-eye. I need to meet with the men and I don't want you underfoot."

Dan wanted to run around a bit and look at the Indians and their camp, but there was no arguing with Jake. He nodded and said, "Yessir, I'll go there now."

As he walked toward Black Bird's tipi, he heard Jake say, "I'll come and fetch you in a couple of hours, okay?"

Dan stopped, turned around and started to say, "Sure thing, sir," but a huge yawn took the place of words. He waved, stumbled in sudden fatigue and wondered, *I didn't know I was so tuckered out so, how did Jake?*

He stepped inside the tipi, made his way blearily toward the back and fell onto a pile of furs, asleep before he even laid his head down.

Chapter Six

DANIEL MONROE SLEPT LONG AND HARD UNTIL FIRST light the next morning. He woke only once as he sensed, rather than felt, Jake join him on the furs sometime in the middle of the night. He remembered hearing drums and distant shouts as if a party was going on in the camp, but he was too exhausted to get up and investigate. He simply snugged up against his mentor and drifted back to sleep.

Coming awake now, he lay gazing up at the hole on top of Black Bird's tipi that let thin trails of wood smoke out into the morning air. His arm was out from under the fur he'd pulled up to his chin while asleep, and he realized it was freezing. He shivered, pulled the covers up and looked over at the others in the tipi.

He saw Black Bird and Green Willow Woman, the teenager, and three, younger children lying together on the other side of the fire. He heard the morning birds' tentative chirps and the sound of the Indian camp stirring in the pre-dawn light.

Sitting up, he yawned and rubbed his eyes. Just as he was about to go outside for nature's call, he felt Jake's large, warm hand clasp his wrist. "Just go out behind the tipi, okay? Don't go into the trees unless someone's with you."

"Yes, sir," Dan mumbled and made his way to the flap. Stepping outside, he saw mist rising off the ground and dancing in the air like haints at a square dance. He walked around the tipi and let loose, sighing with relief. A moment later, Jake joined him.

"I have a few coffee beans left," he said softly. "Let's make breakfast and I'll show you how to shoot a bow."

Dan looked up at Jake with a grin. Three times on their way here Jake had pulled a huge, wicked-looking bow from the back of his saddle and brought game down for them to eat. One was a small, Mule deer buck; one a long, lean Jackrabbit, which tasted like saddle leather and was just about as easy to chew, and the last were two fat grouse. Dan had watched Jake's arrow go through both birds at once.

Dan was hooked. He yearned to know how to shoot a bow and arrow—they were easy to carry, soundless, and just as deadly as any rifle. He'd asked Jake, more than once to teach him after watching the man bag Black Bird with one shot and the second time he asked, Jake handed his bow over.

"Let's see if you can pull that gut-string over. If you can, I'll start teaching you right now," he'd said.

Dan took the bow and was shocked at how big, and heavy it was. He suddenly knew that he was not nearly big enough or strong enough to use Jake's bow, but he gave it his best shot. Jake helped him as best he could… "Back straight! Shoulders back! Set your feet!"

But, try as he might, Dan could not pull the string back more than six to eight inches before getting stuck in mid-pull. After about fifteen minutes of straining until every muscle in his body trembled, Dan gave it up as a job beyond his ability. "I can't budge it, sir." he muttered, handing the bow back to its owner.

Jake studied him for a moment, and said, "This is the wrong bow for you, kid. Way too big, wide and heavy. One of these days, maybe I'll find you a bow you can learn on."

Dan remembered those words now and asked, "Did you find me a bow I can pull, sir?"

Jake nodded. "Yup. Did a little trading last night while you were snoring. Come on, we'll build up Black Bird's fire, have some chow and I'll give you some bow lessons."

Excited and truly happy for the first time in weeks, Dan followed Jake around to the cook fire in front of the tipi and helped his companion build up the fire. Then, Jake brought a smaller, well-worn bow over to him and said, "Try to pull this one over."

Jake stood up, straightened his back, squared his shoulders and pulled. It was almost comically easy. Before, with Jake's bow, he had pulled and pulled until he was sure he was going to pull a muscle, but now he reached the guts zenith with one try and bent the wood just enough to put tension on a nocked arrow… if he had one, which he didn't.

Looking up at Jake, Dan said, "When can I try with an arrow?"

Jake eyed him and answered, "Not now, but soon. First we eat."

It was last night's stew again, and a tad bit mealy but Dan ate it with good appetite. He hadn't realized how good of a cook his ma was, and he had often complained about her dry Dutch oven biscuits and the sameness of every meal, but that was before Jake's rapid race across the northern plains with little food, and before he'd ever had a chance to thank her for all she'd done to make their cross-country trek as safe and easy as possible.

Suddenly tears pricked his eyes again. He knew he wasn't a bad boy, but he *had* been sassy sometimes and ungrateful for the love and shelter his ma and pa had provided him and his brother.

Abruptly, Dan lost his appetite and set the trencher of food down. Jake watched him wipe tears from his face and ask, "May I go for some privacy now, sir?"

Jake nodded, but warned, "Don't go too far, Dan. The critters are out and about this time of day. I don't want to find you et by a grizzly bear."

Dan stared at the trees that still wore cloaks of fog and shivered. Still, he wanted to do his business in private, and wanted to mourn his family without those keen, green eyes watching his every move. "I'll be careful, sir, and I'll be back soon."

"Okay, Dan. I'll be here waiting." Only when the boy disappeared into the tree line did he nod at his nephew, Long Knife, who had been standing quietly to the side of the tipi.

The teenager dipped his head in agreement and headed after Dan to keep watch on his uncle's young charge.

Chapter Seven

LONG KNIFE SAT HIDDEN FROM SIGHT ON A FALLEN LOG and watched Daniel stumble out from behind a large pine tree. He had apparently done his business and was now weeping as if his heart was breaking.

Long Knife had sat up the night before with the men in his tribe and listened as his uncle by marriage confessed to his many misdeeds and spoke of how he had come across the young white boy. He hadn't wanted to be burdened with the kid but couldn't bear the thought of seeing him die out on that endless dusty prairie, abandoned and alone. He had asked the tribe for help and offered many fine guns, knives, and ammunition in return for a couple of weeks' worth of protection and safety.

Long Knife knew of his uncle's kind nature and of his casual cruelties. And, he loved the man despite the fact he had left the village soon after Jake's wife and

Long Knife's older sister Moon Flower and their baby boy had died.

It was no one's fault, really. Moon Flower and her son had simply fallen ill from some sort of flux and died. But Jake had taken it personally, as if all the forces of nature had conspired against his newfound, fragile joy. After the love of his life died, Jake flew into a rage; blaming traveling fur traders, white settlers, other Indian tribes, the tribe's medicine man, and even the moon above for taking his woman and son away.

Finally, inconsolable, he had ridden away from camp and spent the next two and a half years drowning his sorrow in whiskey and debauchery. Long Knife had felt angry and betrayed when his uncle left but he also knew that Jake had endured a life of hardship before becoming a part of his tribe.

As a boy, he, like Daniel Monroe was left alone to die after Sioux Indians set upon his folk's prairie schooner along the Overland Trail west of Scotts Bluff. He had survived to become one with Long Knife's band of Northern Cheyenne that had found him wandering dazed and starving on Wyoming's eastern plains. They had given him food and shelter and eventually, adopted him as their own but it hadn't been an easy life for him.

He had almost died twice—once from a rattlesnake bite and another time from a gunshot sustained in a battle against Custer—the Son of the Morning Star. The band of Indians who had saved him—almost forty-eight in number—was reduced now to only twenty-two members, and they were always on the run—

always one step ahead of the white settlers, and their ever-increasing armies.

Jake had had a hard life and losing Moon Flower and his baby boy was the last straw. Long Knife and his fellow tribe members mourned Jake's loss but had finally moved on without him. Now, though, Jake had come back to them and the teenager's heart was glad.

He understood why his uncle had saved young Daniel—it must be like seeing his younger self, lost and alone, all over again. Still... Long Knife's eyes narrowed as he watched the boy weep. Here was another burden—a white burden—the son of people who seemed bent on destroying all Indians and their way of life.

In addition, he acknowledged he was jealous of the boy. After Moon Flower had died, Long Knife had done his best to fill the hole in his uncle's heart with love but had been rebuffed.

Jake would have been shocked had he known—he simply hadn't noticed his nephew's presence and even if he had, there was no room for love in a heart filled with so much hate and anger.

Still, Long Knife had seen Jake's eyes settle on the youngster with a mixture of frustration, pride and affection and it made him want to bury his newly acquired battle ax right between the boy's wide blue eyes.

But, he had to give the child credit. Dan hadn't laughed when he'd boldly took ahold of his uncle's damn, stubborn old horse, as his friends would have.

Instead, he had hidden his grin and handed Long Knife the grass treat, he should have thought of by himself.

That showed honor—and intelligence. And, the fact the he mourned the loss of his family alone, away from prying eyes spoke of courage.

Long Knife sighed. While Jake and Dan were here, he would protect the boy and maybe teach him how to survive in the wilderness. After that, it was up to his uncle Jake, and the man's capricious whims.

Chapter Eight

TEN DAYS PASSED, AND IN THAT TIME, DAN LEARNED how to shoot a bow and arrow, rifle and pistol. He met most of the tribe members and learned a little of their lingo. He paid close attention to their many hand signals, as a universal language amongst the many plains Indians was nonexistent. The Indians not only approved their sovereignty, they encouraged it. Still, it was important to have a rudimentary communal language; and out on these vast inland plains, sign language was the key.

He was even introduced to the chief. After several lectures about being respectful, and *keeping his mouth shut*, he was led to the fire in front of the villages largest tipi, and watched as an ancient old man, accompanied by three equally ancient women, his wives, made their way out of the tipi and sat down by the fire. The chief, whose name was Iron Horse grinned toothlessly at Dan from across the fire and made a motion in the air. Immediately, one of the women unwrapped a soft leather bundle and pulled a pipe from its folds.

His voice was creaky from lack of use, but he spoke to Jake, who repeated the oldster's words for Dan to hear. "We are sorry to hear that your people died at the hands of bandits. Those groups of bad men thrive here in the desert, like grasshoppers in the sun." He lit his pipe and took two or three long pulls. Then, he handed the pipe to one of his wives and gestured in Dan's direction.

The old woman got slowly to her feet and offered the pipe to Dan, who took it and glanced up at Jake for directions.

Jake grinned, "Iron Horse offers you a great honor. Take a small puff, maybe two, and then give the pipe back to Brown Feather. Go easy, kid, that pipe packs a wallop."

"Yes, sir" Dan murmured and took a small puff off the beautiful, elaborately carved pipe. Not knowing what to expect, he took another, longer puff and handed the pipe back to Brown Feather. He started to climb to his feet to pay his respects, but his head grew light, and he started to cough.

It was as if the small amount of smoke he'd inhaled suddenly quadrupled in size and exploded in his lungs. His face turned as red as a beet as he wheezed and snorted, trying to clear his nasal passages, and through streaming tear-filled eyes he saw the rest of the Indians gathered around him glance at one another, while trying to hide their grins of amusement.

Jake pounded him on the back and Dan heard him say, "Easy, kid, you'll be alright. Shoot, I thought I told you to go easy…"

Then, as quickly as it had come, the effect of the pipes fumes mellowed, and his lungs were able to draw air again. He felt better now but changed as well. Everything seemed etched in light, and his muscles felt like they were made of *caoutchouc*, or rubber.

He studied the Indians sitting around him and suddenly felt as if he understood what they were saying —maybe not the words they spoke but the meaning behind those words.

The old chief spoke again. "Welcome to the people, foster son of our foster son. You will find succor in our camp for as long as I take breath."

Jake whispered the chief's words in his ear and Dan heard Iron Horse's three wives repeat his blessing. Then, baskets of food were passed around—heavy pan bread torn into small pieces, strips of buffalo meat, and a basket of berries so purple and fragrant, Dan couldn't imagine anything tasting as sweet ever again.

Turning to his right, he smiled at Long Knife and held up a hand stained blue with the berries juice. "Good! Really good, Knife!"

Long Knife smiled and nodded. The boy's eyes were bright red and barely focused. He had drawn deeply of old Grandfather's pipe, and would need to rest soon, but he couldn't help but feel proud of the kid and his effort to stay awake.

Daniel had taken to his lessons with keen enthusiasm and had become as good of a shot as Long Knife in the short time he'd been here. *He's good with the fire sticks, too, better than I will ever be,* Long Knife thought with a sigh of disgust.

His uncle had told him, more than once, if he was going to protect the tribe, he would need to learn the white man's ways, including the weapons they bore. But one of Long Knife's earliest and most terrifying memories was of white soldiers led by a mad man with long, red hair named Custer, who killed men, women and children by the score with those rifles, pistols and muzzle-loaders—sticks of fire and thunder that could tear a body into pieces with one loud bang.

Even now, as a full-grown man, he often woke up at night with a shout of fright and a pounding heart, only to find himself lying amongst his own people, safe from harm. The only witness to his fear; his father whose dark, steady eyes gazed at him in the fire's soft glow.

Chapter Nine

JAKE AND DAN LEFT THE CHEYENNE CAMP TWO DAYS later, and it looked like the Indians were fixing to move on, as well. The giant pile of buffalo skins, hides, and bones was reduced to chow for the camps many dogs now, and dozens of temporary drying racks were being rebuilt into dozens of travois.

Dan was proud to know he had done his part in helping his new Indian friends process the buffalo they needed to survive the swiftly approaching winter season. He had helped in scraping blood, meat, gristle and fat off the hides, and rendered the bladders into viable drinking containers.

He had helped the women pick through the bones, boil them until they were as white as snow, and turn the choicest bits into cutlery, needles, tomahawk blades and trenchers.

He ate well, slept like a log and eventually put his grief aside, accepting the fact that his life was irrevocably changed. When he wasn't helping his Indian hosts, he spent his time with Jake and his new friend, Long Knife.

The teenager was a poor conversationalist but managed to communicate with Dan through sign language and example. He was patient and helpful in teaching Dan how to comport himself in the wilderness.

He learned how to throw a hatchet and an awl. Eventually, after showing much promise, Long Knife allowed him to throw his own precious battle-axe. It was beautifully balanced and had been presented to Knife on his sixteenth birthday as a rite of passage into manhood. Whenever he and Knife set up targets to throw their axes at, Knife's friends would appear out of nowhere like magic.

It seemed to Dan like axe work was all the rage for these youngsters, and many elaborate contests were staged for these competitions. Dan never won, but he was as proud as a rooster when some of his throws landed true, and the other boys cheered his efforts.

Then, it was time to leave. Jake had grown distant again and seemed in a big hurry to whisk Dan away to yet another life. When the older man was happy, his wide grin and green eyes seemed to glow with warmth, but when he grew sad, those same eyes seemed as chill as a deep mountain brook, depthless and deadly.

Dan helped Jake pack up the horses, and then followed the older man back into the heart of the camp where many of Jake's friends and family stood waiting.

Black Bird, Green Willow Woman and Long Knife stood by the chief's fire with bundles of food, some medicine paste, and two fur capes—gifts given to Jake and his charge for the winter to come.

Jake said little but accepted the gifts with grace. Then, he hugged Long Knife, his mother-in-law, and clasped arms with his father-in-law, before turning to old Iron Horse, bowing slightly and saying formal words of thanks and goodbye.

Dan just stood there, feeling inadequate and regretful that they had to leave at all. He felt that, given time, he could learn the Cheyenne way and make a home among these fine people. But, Jake clearly had other ideas and was, even now, turning away to mount up. Dan gave an awkward wave, said, "Bye!" and ran after Jake who seemed ready to leave, with or without him.

As he and Jake took their leave, Dan turned around in his saddle and took one last look at the Indian encampment. Long Knife stood staring back at him, but the rest of the village went about their business, packing their meager belongings in preparation for their trek south.

Then the trees blocked his vision and he turned around to face what was to come.

———

THEY STAYED in the trees for the next three days and nights. There was, for the most part, a clear trail to follow so the horses were not in peril from fallen trees, sticks, branches and hidden pitfalls. But it was slow going, and Jake had not shed his bad mood since the morning they'd left the Indian camp.

Dan was feeling ill at ease. He was back to wondering if Jake had changed his mind about dragging him along and couldn't help but wonder if he was even safe with this cold and distant stranger.

Finally, on the fourth morning traveling northward, Dan asked, "Sir, mind if I ask where we're going?"

Jake started a little as though he'd forgotten that he even had a traveling partner. But for the first time in days, Dan was relieved to see a slight twinkle in the man's eyes.

"We're heading to my house. Hopefully, it's still there." Jake said.

"I didn't know you had your own home, sir. I guess I thought that home for you meant the Cheyenne..."

Jake nodded. "You're right about that but my wife and I had our own place. It's not much, but it's mine. I was thinking you could stay with me a while and help me make it livable again. Maybe help me bring in some meat for the winter... looks to me like we're in for a long one."

Dan stared at his traveling companion and saw that the recent storm in Jake's heart seemed to have passed. Jake's face was clear and bright again and his smile gleamed like sunlight through dark clouds.

Jake glanced at Dan, adding, "That's only if you're of a mind to... if you'd rather, I'll ride most of the way to the closest town with you. It's about fifty-miles away from here. I haven't got much money set by, but I think I have enough to get you sitting pretty at an orphanage..."

"NO!" Dan blurted. "I mean... please sir, let me stay with you, okay? I promise I'll be good and won't give you no sass. I'll work hard and help you... I promise!"

Jake stared at Dan with surprise. The kid was literally trembling with fear and dread at being left alone. He knew he was rough company and had thought that being given an alternative would be appreciated, but even now, tears of fright were welling up in Dan's eyes.

Jake's thought about it. It would be a good thing to have help in the long winter months ahead, and if Dan didn't mind his occasional dark spells, maybe he'd even dull the loneliness of being cooped up for months on end. Seeing the devastation in the kid's face, he nodded.

"Okay then. You can stay with me—for a while, at least."

Chapter Ten

1877

THREE YEARS HAD PASSED like a slow dream. Twelve-year-old Daniel Monroe sat on a log with his feet in the water and his hands working along the sandy edges of the river's bank. He was "trout tickling" and had already caught three fat fish for tonight's supper.

He was enjoying a rare day off from chores, lessons and the steady work of keeping alive in the southern Rockies. Jake was out on his own this day, checking his trap lines. Come tomorrow, Dan knew he would be busy skinning and cleaning the beaver, mink and otter Jake had caught but for now, he was content to loll around in the sun and take stock of his life.

Gazing across a wild-flower dotted meadow, he stared at Jake's house and was satisfied. Remembering back to when he'd first followed Jake to his abandoned home, he saw what the place looked like now, and marveled at the changes.

Jake's house *had* been little more than a shallow stone cave covered over with scraped log walls and canvas tarps which were torn into frayed, flapping strips. The lodgepole pine cross-pieces of the corral in front of the shelter had mostly fallen to the ground leaving only the fence posts standing half-cocked and jagged like crooked teeth.

It looked forlorn and abandoned, much like Dan himself, and he immediately fell in love with the sad little house that was nestled into a green valley between two high mountain peaks.

Jake, who had just recently come out of one of his funks, grinned at the sight of his homestead. Turning to Dan, he said, "I was afeared someone might have moved in here. I got papers on the place, but they're tucked into a safety-deposit box at a bank in Laramie. Lot of times, possession carries more sand than paper."

Jake kicked his horse into a trot and Dan followed. They tied their horses' reins on the corrals fence-posts and walked to the house. They ducked under the torn tarps and stepped inside. Looking around at the rubble-strewn mess that had once been home for him and his family Jake sighed, and that familiar darkness filled his heart.

Red gingham curtains were lying in a pile on the dirt floor from the one window Jake had built into the chinked logs and the kitchen table had fallen over, victim of a broken leg. Shelves, filled with jugs, broken clay jars and dusty metal tins graced the right wall. A rusty woodstove sat cold and dark by the front corner.

Jake saw the wreck of his previous happy life within the confines of the log hut, but Dan was delighted. "Looks like we could use some new sod for the roof, sir. You want me to cut some out?" he asked his companion.

Jake stared down at the kid's happy face and made a determined effort to pull himself out of the past. "You can do that tomorrow. Right now, let's get this place cleaned up…"

They swept through the old log house, throwing most everything out in the weed-infested front yard. Then, Jake threw the shutters open for light while Dan cleaned the stove and chimney pipe.

As Dan brought in wood and kindling for a fire, Jake replaced the table's broken leg with a stout branch. Then, he moved over to the wall of shelves and poked around in the tins, finding some moldy flour, stale coffee beans and more importantly, some rusty red kidney beans. He bit into one and nodded. They were fine to eat and ready for the cook pot.

He blew dust and spider webs, including one occupant; out of the cast-iron kettle and walked outside to fetch water from a small creek that skirted his property. He filled the pot with water and took a moment to stare about. The dark mood that was threatening to over-whelm him receded as he saw the golden, shimmering aspens growing along the creek banks, and the green fir trees and red-fingered Tamarack ringing his land.

Jake took three deep breaths to clear his mind and brought the water inside to cook the beans while he and the boy unpacked the horses and began to build a new life for themselves.

————

DAN DECIDED to stop fishing and go check on his own three traps, but first, he wanted to eat his lunch. He pulled a tiny green apple, and a couple of pieces of jerky out of his kit and stared at the house again. It was practically unrecognizable from what it had been when he'd first arrived.

The log façade had been rebuilt and chinked. The corral had also been built up and was now much larger and taller. They had cobbled together a small barn and the front yard was neat and tidy. Four horses, one mean old mule, two Guernsey milk cows, three broods and six longhorn cattle grazed the valley's pasture.

Dan had asked where the horseflesh and cattle came from, but Jake's face told the tale—*Don't ask, and I won't have to lie*, his expression said, and by now Dan knew better than to pry. At any rate, the ramshackle homestead was a going concern now, and Dan took pride in his hard work making it so.

He remembered their first winter here and shivered. Jake and Dan had holed up in the cave behind the house most of those first five months, and they had brought the horses in with them. One night, Jake announced, "Ye know, that wagon train you rode in never woulda made it…"

Dan's head jerked up. He thought of his lost family most every day but had started to think of Jake as his new pa—a sullen, often melancholy father figure to be sure, but very much alive, and always ready to show him how to survive these wild mountains.

Jake had stopped talking and stared toward the house proper—at the cold woodstove, the empty shelves and sacks of hard tack and grain that acted as a wall against the frigid temperatures outside.

"Why's that, sir?" Dan ventured.

Jake turned toward him with angry eyes and snarled, "Why, that teamster didn't know his ass from a teakettle, that's why! When did you and your folks light out from Kentucky, anyway?"

"Uh…" Dan gulped. He hated it when Jake got like this; sad, remorseful, always simmering like a pot on a slow boil. "I think it was the middle of July, sir. Don't hardly remember the date."

Jake nodded, "See—that was *way* too late for taking a train over the Rockies or the Sierra Nevada's! You woulda all died in the winter snows!"

Dan sat still with his mouth hanging open. Jake had stood up by now and was bent over yelling at him, as if *he* were that ill-advised wagon master. His eyes were white-ringed and wild, and Dan could tell that the man's cheekbones sported bright red circles of fury.

He wanted to object… Old Whitey Humphreys had

seemed like a pretty good hand to Dan, and he'd always had a comforting Bible passage at hand and an endless supply of hard rock candy for the sprouts in his train. *Besides,* Dan thought resentfully. *Humphreys is dead now and it hardly seems fair of Jake to cast aspersions on the man's character, now that he isn't around to defend himself.*

For the first time ever, Dan was ready to open his mouth and say something disrespectful to Jake but before he could, the man toppled over and fell in a moaning heap on the stone floor.

Dan shook his head now, recalling just how close he'd come to losing his adopted father over the next few weeks. Somewhere along the way, Jake had picked up a chill and it had turned into pneumonia. Somehow, as the snow blew in a howling frenzy outside, and drifted up the walls of the house to a depth of over five feet, Dan nursed Jake back to health.

And, thank the good Lord above, Dan sighed. He knew he wouldn't have survived that first terrible winter alone and since then he and Jake had become close. Sure, the man had his dark moods and he was a fierce task-master, but he was also kind, courteous and surprisingly well-educated.

Dan's eyes started to close as the hot August sun fell over his body like a blanket. Crickets sounded their castanets, and Dan's body relaxed into a light doze. Then, his eyes flew open as he heard the jaws of his steel-trap snap shut and the pained squeal of whatever his trap had just caught.

Chapter Eleven

DAN HAD LAID HIS TRAPS ON THE OPPOSITE SIDE OF THE creek every one-hundred-feet or so, and he thought one of the furthest traps had sprung shut. He jumped to his feet and picked up the shotgun Jake had given him a year earlier. It was old, and too heavy for him, but he loved it. It had been corroded, rusty, and etched with three strange letters—G T T.

When Jake presented the shotgun to him, Dan had asked, "What do these letters mean, sir?"

Jake leaned over and saw that Dan had cleared years of accumulated grime away from the wooden stock and the letters he had once etched into the wood showed clearly. That was a long time ago, though, and even now those memories stung. He stood up, and spat, "Nuthin', Dan. Those letters don't mean nuthin', no more. Keep a cleanin'."

NOW, as he ran toward the beaver colony that had sprung up during last spring's thaw, he hoped that the buck in that colony had met his sorry end. Normally, Dan had a kindly disposition toward God's creatures, but he and that danged old buck beaver had declared war on one another over the last few months.

More than once, as Dan set his traps, that buck had launched itself into the creek, big square teeth bared in a rictus grin, and chased him back to the shoreline. Then it would hiss and growl and smack its tail on the water to protect the females and kits in their lodge.

Once, Dan had swam too close and the beast had sunk its teeth into one of his moccasins, practically nipping his little toe off in the process, before swimming back to the dam with a triumphant, high-pitched whistle as its fellows sat on their haunches and watched.

Notwithstanding his fury, Dan was also embarrassed when Jake saw the damage done to his foot and moccasin. First, he had inspected the gouge marks on Dan's foot and after a thorough inspection, he burst into laughter. He laughed so hard tears sprang from his eyes and he slapped his knees in mirth.

Dan was aghast. "Why're you laughing, sir? That thing nearly bit my foot off!" he exclaimed.

Settling down, Jake wiped his eyes, and sat down across from him in their now, cozy kitchen. "Look, kid. Everything; whether ye be man or beast, loves something. Just 'because you are a human, don't make you better—or even smarter—than the animals you hunt."

He gazed into Dan's indignant eyes, and continued, "You just got taught a lesson, son. Respect the animals you hunt—they got every right to protect what's theirs. Take care—and honor them. They don't want to lose their hides or be lowered into the cook pot, and they will fight to survive—just like we do."

He took a gentle hold on Dan's foot, and then started scrubbing the bite marks with a sudsy, wet rag. "Ouch!" Dan hollered, but Jake gritted his teeth and snarled, "We gotta do this, Dan. I doubt it, but that critter may have had hydrophobia... best not take any chances."

———

DAN HAD ENDURED THE ENCOUNTER, but he still felt resentment toward that buck and hoped he'd find the ornery animal in his trap. He waded across the creek, holding his shotgun up out of the water and saw a furious scuffle taking place by his trap.

He squinted into the gloom trying to make sense of the battle going on under the tree's shadows and stepped up out of the water. Dan took three or four cautious steps and saw that indeed; the buck beaver had sprung the trap and was fighting something off.

Then he gasped and took a step back as his nemesis suddenly squealed in pain as it was shaken violently from side to side. Then, it fell over dead, its throat torn out. Dan felt a moment's sympathy. He had hated that nasty old buck, but it was a worthy opponent. Now, it would protect its lodge no longer.

He only had a second to grieve, though, as the attacking animal turned around and showed itself.

It's a skunk bear!, Dan realized in horror before the wolverine sprang through the air and attached itself to his face and neck; nothing but teeth, claws and feral fury.

Chapter Twelve

JAKE HAD JUST RETURNED HOME AND WAS PLEASED WITH his bountiful harvest. He had bagged seven fat beaver and surprisingly, two mink that had approached the trap together and unfortunately, were trapped and killed together as well.

He figured that he and Dan had enough plews and other furs and hides to make a good trade in the booming railroad town of Laramie, Wyoming Territory, two months from now. Meanwhile, he and the kid had been lucky this year in making meat. They had shot and processed more than a dozen deer, five elk, and one black bear that was good for its fur as well as the fat and tallow it brought to their stores.

All the meat had been salted and cured and was piled up in plenty at the back of the stone cavern. They had enough meat left over to trade with some of their distant neighbors for hay and grain, which was stored in the small barn. He and Dan had also traded some of their better furs for beans, coffee, sugar and cold-storage vegetables like corn, beans, onions and potatoes.

Not once, since he'd purchased his property had the creek run dry, and although some of the shallower depths froze over during the winter there were plenty of small, deep pools that ran fresh and clear even in the coldest months and provided him and his foster son with trout and bass. He stared out at his small homestead with a smile of accomplishment and pride on his face. God willing, he and Dan would survive another winter, and he was satisfied.

Then his eyes narrowed as he spied the boy stumbling through the meadow with both hands covering his face. Dan weaved drunkenly, and Jake thought he heard a moaning cry cutting through the sleepy, afternoon sounds of cricket and bird song.

His old packhorse, Jonesy, who had developed a deep affection for the kid and followed him around like a lap dog, lifted his head, nickered and ran toward the stumbling figure. So, did Jake.

He threw his hat to the ground and bolted across the meadow, scattering the mule and some of the steers. Getting to within about 20-feet, Jake saw that blood was trickling through Dan's fingers, and running in red sheets down his arms. Dan must have sensed his approach, because it was as if all the strength abruptly left his legs and he fell to his knees in shock and pain.

"Pa? Is that you? I'm... I'm hurt."

Jake paused, and his heart gave a painful lurch. Only

once had the boy ever called him Pa, and that was when he was in the grip of a burning fever. A traveling trader named Boss Chew had brought medicinal supplies; alcohol, assorted trinkets like needles, buttons, cloth, nails, thread, boots and shoes, and farming utensils such as shovels and rakes in his wagon. He had stayed the night in their barn, broke bread with them and brought them news from the outside world.

It was a fine visit and Jake liked the old trader with his far-gazing eyes, long gray hair and colorful stories. But this time, old Boss had unknowingly carried the measles with him as well. Jake had survived the same rash when he was a child and was now immune to its affects, but Dan was stricken hard.

He had alternately baked with a high fever and shivered with chill as his young body bloomed with fiery, red spots. Once, during his illness, he had stared up at Jake with glazed eyes and said, "Pa, is that you? Oh, I've missed you..."

At that moment, Jake despaired. He thought it was the end of the road for his young charge—he could feel heat coming off his body like a cook stove—but the next morning the fever broke and a few days later, although he was still covered in itchy, red bumps, Dan was hungry and antsy to get up and go outside. He'd never called Jake 'Pa' again.

Now, Jake ran up to where Dan was lying on the grass. "Dan... Dan! Give up yore arms and let me see!" he ordered, but the boy clamped his hands even tighter, sending fresh rosettes of blood seeping through his fingers.

"Dan, leave off, dammit!" Jake growled and pulled the boy's hands away. Then, he sat back with a sigh. "Whooo, boy. What did this?"

Dan's right cheek hung in a tattered flap off his cheekbone and the left side of his face sported three long, bloody gashes. Luckily, both of his eyes were intact, and there were no deep tears by his jugular. He would live to tell the tale but would have some serious scars to show for it.

"Gulo, Gulo, sir. I was... I was checking the trap... and..." Dan passed-out from shock and blood loss.

Jake shook his head. Dan was growing up to be quite the looker with his fair skin, bright blue eyes and glossy black hair. He'd seen some of the young neighbor girls staring at the boy with wide, dreamy eyes and their Momma's speculative appraisals.

He picked Dan up in his arms and carried him back to the house, while Jonesy followed. He was happy to have bought a new set of needles this last spring. And relieved that he had been taught to sew by the men of the Cheyenne, who didn't do a lot of housekeeping but were very good at stitch-work.

He sighed in disgust, thinking that sometimes this kid was more trouble than he was worth. Jake always had to worry over the boy's welfare and he was another mouth to feed. Dan was growing like a weed too, which meant he sometimes needed to eat more than his fair share! *Nuthin' but trouble*, he grumbled.

He had a big job ahead of him tonight, not to mention a lot of painful administration. Dan was sure to wake up once Jake's needles pierced his flesh, and he wouldn't be happy nor comfortable with the painful process. *But, that's just too bad*, Jake thought.

He would do whatever was necessary to keep the boy breathing and able to face the world as an adult. Just because *he* had been left alone as a boy and had to find his own way in a hostile land, didn't mean that Dan had to go it alone. Not while Jake was still breathing.

As the older man walked toward his home and kicked his way through a few laying hens in the front yard with the boy in his arms, it never occurred to him that the feelings in his heart were the very definition of love.

Chapter Thirteen

IT TOOK A LONG TIME FOR THE BOY TO HEAL, BOTH physically and emotionally. Although Jake did a good job stitching Dan's face, the torn flesh became infected and he was forced to use leeches, and a foul-smelling concoction his Cheyenne family had given him as they traveled through the area last spring.

The paste was made by the tribe's medicine man and consisted of rancid bear fat, Goldenseal, Cone Flower petals and hot peppers. Just applying it to Dan's wounds made Jake's eyes water and triggered his sneeze reflex, but the boy howled at the sting of it, and begged Jake to leave off torturing him.

Finally, after three agonizing weeks, the infection passed, and Dan was able to rest and heal from the wolverine's attack. He asked Jake once, "Do you think I got the distemper, sir?"

Although he had used as much hot soap, water and whiskey as he'd dared, Jake had no way of knowing, and he shrugged. "Don't know, Dan. You haven't showed any symptoms, but sometimes the signs don't show up for years."

Dan's eyes studied his face and the fear in them was obvious. Jake added, "You know how I said that some animals show they're sick by biting and growling… they are thirsty but too sick to drink. They foam at the mouth?"

Dan nodded, imagining himself in a similar state, and shuddered. Jake saw his reaction and added, "Well, wolverines are just naturally mean. They will come after just about anything, even if it's three times their size. They bite and growl all the time and most animals steer clear, cuz they're plumb crazy."

A couple of tears leaked from the kid's eyes, and Jake concluded by saying, "What I mean to say is, you tangled with the wrong critter. That skunk bear might have seemed crazy sick but that's just its natural condition. Put those fearful thoughts of hydrophobia out of yore mind and just concentrate on getting better, okay?"

About a week later, Dan had regained his feet and was doing some light chores around the place like rolling their many plews into easy to carry bundles, cleaning the house, fetching in the eggs and filling the livestock's water trough. It was also wash-up day and Dan spent an hour and a half bringing buckets of water into the house to warm for bathing.

Jake came into the house at twilight and started pulling his boots and clothes off for his weekly bath.

He looked up at Dan who was ladling venison stew into bowls for their supper, and saw that steady tears were leaking from the kid's eyes. Shocked, he snapped, "What the hell's wrong with you?"

Used to this kind of reaction from Jake toward undue displays of emotion, Dan gingerly wiped the tears from his face, shrugged and said, "Nuthin', sir. I'm sorry." He brought the stew and some flat bread over to Jake and went back to the stove to fetch his own dinner.

Jake stared at the boy's back as he walked away and realized Dan had undergone another growth-spurt when he wasn't paying attention. He figured the kid was close to 5'7 and although thin from his injuries and subsequent fevers he was probably a good 160 pounds. He was a handsome young man, tall and straight, and strong as an oak tree.

Just as these thoughts crossed Jake's mind, he heard Dan say, "Guess I'm a monster now…" He tucked into his stew, but Jake saw that new tears threatened. It was true that the kid's right cheek was torn into an unsightly horseshoe shape, stretching from the corner of his mouth to the lower corner of his eye.

Right now, the skin around the gash was swollen and discolored with black, blue, yellow and green bruises. Dan's other cheek was much better, though. The three scratches hadn't been as deep and now just showed three, scabbed-over diagonal lines. The wound on his neck, although worrisome at first, was nearly healed over.

Jake shrugged. "Didn't know you was so vain…" and as soon as those words slipped his tongue, he regretted them. Dan wasn't vain, at all. Although Jake owned a looking glass, he could count on one hand the times Dan had contemplated his own reflection.

Softening his tone, he asked, "Did ye catch sight of yourself, Dan?"

Dan nodded. "Yes sir, fetching water for our bath. I never much cared about what I looked like… figured I must look like you, but I wasn't prepared for how ugly I am now."

Jake gathered his thoughts. He couldn't help but wonder if the boy had forgotten about his own pa, or if he had just replaced the man for Jake in his heart. He also understood just how much of a father figure he had become in the boy's eyes.

Jake cleared his throat and muttered. "I know it looks bad right now, son. But the stitch work is clean, and the infection is gone. Pretty soon the swelling and bruises will fade, too. You just wait—a year from now, that big ole scar will turn white and kinda disappear. A scar like that gives a man character, it don't turn him into a monster. We clear on that?" He stared at Dan's wet face.

"Yes, sir. I ain't a monster."

"Aren't…" Jake mumbled automatically and dipped his spoon into his stew.

Chapter Fourteen

THE MORNING SUN WAS HOT AND BRIGHT, BUT THE breeze that blew through the autumn leaves was chill, promising winter's inevitable arrival. It was the 4th of October 1878 and Daniel was learning how to shoot. He had been looking forward to this for as long as he could remember, but now that it was happening, he was disgusted, disappointed and sore—both in his body and his mind.

Jake had given him one of his old scatterguns, and after several terse instructions, he was placed in front of a series of targets and told to fire away. To Dan's complete humiliation, he missed every single target.

He couldn't understand it! Whenever he went out hunting, he was proud of his shooting skills. Even Jake, always scarce with praise, had nodded in approval whenever he bagged a squirrel, or a rabbit or a grouse with his little .32. He had even brought down a buffalo calf once; a lucky shot that hit the young animal right in the eye, but he could barely hit the side of a barn now.

The shotgun wasn't too difficult. Just aim and you were sure to hit something. Still, that wasn't good enough for his mentor; who frowned and said, "If you drop one of our cattle with that thing, I'm gonna take the cost outta your hide."

So, Dan had lifted the heavy shotgun, took careful aim and managed to blow a bunch of old tins off the top rail of the pasture fence. He smiled and turned to Jake with pride, only to be frowned at and told, "What are ye waiting for? Load up and do it again!"

Dan had done so, until he could barely lift the gun. His ammunition consisted of a powder horn, and soft lead BBs. Jake told him that metal filings, broken-down nails, lead balls and anything else that would fit in the barrel worked as well, but this sort of ammo was hard on the gun and only used in a dire emergency. By the time he was done, his hands and fingers were cut up, his arms were black with smoke and his shoulders trembled with fatigue.

Although Dan hated it, Jake made him practice with that nasty old muzzle-loader for almost a month, before he graduated into working with the Colt pistol. *This is more like it!*, he thought with a grin, when he grabbed the pistol up off the kitchen table that first morning—only to have it immediately snatched from his hand.

"Lookit what yore doing, boy!" Jake thundered.

Dan was sucking on the edge of his thumb with

tears of pain filling his eyes as he stared at Jake. "What? What did I do?"

"You had that pistol aimed right between my eyes, is what!" Jake growled, and Dan recalled that he hadn't really been thinking about the gun or where it was pointed when he'd picked it up. He was only feeling the excitement of finally being able to hold it.

"S...sorry, sir. I wasn't thinking..."

Jake rolled his eyes, and then gave out a little grin. "'Tweren't loaded. Still, this here is a killing tool. I seen more than my fair share of pistol men blow their own parts off just 'because they weren't paying attention to where they was aimin' their guns."

Dan, who was sucking on a large, painful welt creasing the bottom of his right thumb, nodded and said, "Yessir. I'll be more careful from now on."

Jake then proceeded to tell him about the gun, its inception by Mr. Samuel Colt in 1851, its firepower, and the type of ammo it used. He also said, "This here gun is what cost the Confederates the war, ye know. If our side would have been issued these pistols, like the Union boys was, the South woulda won that war, fer sure."

Despite his sore thumb, Dan was eager to get started on it but instead, Jake took the revolver away, wrapped it up in a soft deer hide, and placed a rusty old, Colt Pocket Percussion gun on the table. "Now, I want you to clean this gun up and we'll start you shootin' on it in the morning."

Another muzzle-loader!, Dan thought with a groan.

Seeing the downcast expression on the kid's face, Jake grinned, adding, "Besides, I think you got a nice fat blister comin' on."

Looking down, Dan saw that, indeed, a blister the size of an oak leaf was blossoming on his palm. He sighed in disgust, and grumbled, "You done it to me, sir, when you snatched that revolver away from me...."

Jake nodded in agreement and replied, "Fetch the gun oil down and get started cleaning up that *fine* piece of weaponry." Then he walked outside leaving Dan to brood.

———

IT TOOK the better part of winter of 1878-'79 before Jake was satisfied with Dan's shooting skills. By now, the boy had a fair acquaintance with the revolver, the scattergun and the old ball and powder muzzleloader. He was also developing great arm-strength and muscles for a boy his size. All three weapons were heavy and pistol practice flat-guaranteed a certain amount of muscle-memory and grace.

He was taught how to quick draw and cross draw the Colt .44 to clear leather quickly in a gunfight.

By the time the snows came, smothering their small dwelling in four to five-foot drifts, Dan could hold his own—if push came to shove. Jake did not want the boy to become a gunman or a quick draw artist, but he *did* want Dan to know how to defend himself in a gunfight.

There were too many bad men in the western wilds to survive without shooting skills, and Jake did not want Dan to perish from a lack of preparation. Watching the boy dry-fire the Colt and seeing how fast he had become, Jake nodded his head in approval.

Just as the snows began to wane and spring started to quicken the valley, both Jake and Dan's shooting skills would be put to the test.

Chapter Fifteen

TWO FRENCH TRAPPERS, BERNARD ACHILLES, AND Dominique Etienne; better known as Bo and Dom were running for their lives. One could say that they had been running for their lives since the day they were born. Born to poverty and forced to do whatever it took to survive in Paris, they had spent a good portion of their young adult years in prison for theft, malicious mischief and attempted murder.

During one of the multiple-upheavals to the French government in the 1870s, they gained their freedom and took advantage of the opportunity to leave France as quickly as possible. Having become fast friends in jail they decided to flee together to New Orleans and then St. Louis in the United States. Once there, they might have decided to follow the path of right-eousness... there were opportunities a-plenty, but their rough beginnings had been carved deep, and they found themselves involved in criminal enterprises in

New Orleans before escaping for their lives to St. Louis. After a couple more years of petty crimes and grift along the docks of the rough-and-tumble river town, both men decided they should take their ruinous ways out West before ending up in the river floating all the way to hell back to New Orleans.

In 1879, they signed on with a buffalo hide hunting outfit—mainly for free passage West in exchange for honest labor. From the very beginning, Louis Bertrand, the boss of the outfit, recognized Bo and Dom for the lazy skunks they were, but the trapping party was getting a late start up-river. He needed all the help he could get, even if it was poor help. Plus, he figured he would simply dump the two malingerers in the Wyoming Territory once they got there.

Unfortunately, it didn't work out the way he planned. Once the outfit made Cheyenne, and most of his men were spending time at one the saloons in town, Louis was knocked over the head by the butt of a pistol and had to watch in woozy confusion as Bo and Dom robbed him blind before disappearing north.

The men took three horses loaded up with fur-trapping gear, cookware, guns, knives, food, and what money they could get their hands on. Poor Louis was fired and was fetched back home to St. Louis by two of his sons to heal from his injuries. Four of the other hunters joined other hunting parties, but three of the men were so enraged by the theft of their earthly possessions, they set out after the two French men to retrieve their property.

Which was why Bo and Dom were running now. They had thought they'd gotten away clean, but after two days of hard riding, they realized they were being pursued. Like a pesky cloud of skeeters, three men rode after them relentlessly—day and night.

Bo suggested they surrender part of their stolen goods, thinking this would pacify their pursuers, which it did somewhat, but not nearly enough for them to call off the chase.

Miles flew by as Bo and Dom were harried until they found themselves leaving the grassy plains behind and making their way up the rock-covered and ice-scrimmed foothills of the southern Rockies. Dom could not read and didn't care to learn how, but his friend Bo could and had one read that the Rocky Mountains were as high as the sky and practically endless.

They were perilous too, of course, especially during the winter months, but it was coming onto spring now. He figured the best way to lose their enemies was to head on up and hide in the vast wilderness of forest, cliffs and bluffs. Dom was intimidated by the snow-covered peaks but was also tired of being on the run and trusted his friend enough to let Bo lead the way.

They spent the better part of a day picking their way up a goat path on the side of a mountain and got a birds-eye view of their enemies exiting a copse of trees and galloping their horses across the long green valley from which they'd ridden that morning. One of the men owned a spyglass, and Bo saw the sparkle of sun on glass as the man searched the hillside he and Dom were on.

Then, even as high up as they were by now, both men heard their followers whoop and holler in glee as they were discovered. But...

Bo frowned. There was whoopin' and hollering going on for sure, but he didn't think those cries of triumph came from the men he and Dom had robbed. Turning in his saddle, Bo's mouth sagged open in shock as he saw a large band of Indians converging on their pursuers.

There were at least twenty-five braves riding toward their former colleagues, and he watched as the three men turned their horses around and tried to flee back toward the western tree line. But they were too slow and far out-numbered.

Bo and Dom got down off their horses, crawled on their bellies to a large mound of brush, and watched as the men were surrounded, pin-cushioned by countless arrows, and finally scalped.

Then the Indians scavenged what little the men had left and stole their horses. As they exited the valley to the east, Bo and Dom saw the natives gazing around with keen eyes, and they ducked their heads as the Indian's gaze raked the slopes they were perched on.

Several breathless moments passed, and then Bo opened his eyes and peered down into the lush green valley. The Indians were gone, and the only thing left of their pursuers was dead meat—which would soon be dinner for the carrion birds circling overhead.

Scooting backwards, he murmured, "We must be going, Dommie. Those Injuns may circle back and put us on the menu next, *oui?*"

They found their horses grazing on spring grass about thirty-yards away, mounted up and headed north.

Chapter Sixteen

BO AND DOM WERE LOUSY SHOTS, AND NEITHER ONE HAD learned how to trap, so things became dicey for them in short order. By this time; eight days after they'd fled Cheyenne, their supplies were running short. Their coffee was gone, as was all the hardtack, and most of the flour. There were only enough beans for two small meals.

They needed meat but every rabbit they spotted got away clean, and the one bull elk that stood broadside to them, as though begging to be shot, walked away and out of sight in arrogant leisure as both men missed... although they'd had all the time in the world to reload and shoot again.

They had just brushed themselves off from that humiliating encounter when Dom spotted a moose molesting the bottom branches of a fir tree. He knelt on the frozen ground, took careful aim and let fly—

only to have the gigantic animal turn, stare at them, let out a furious bawling sound and run straight at them.

Dom fell over backwards and climbing to his feet with a bellow of fear, followed Bo who was running as fast as his feet would carry him. Dom's heart skipped a beat as he glanced over his shoulder and saw that the beast was gaining on him—her giant hoofbeats shaking the very ground he ran on.

"Bo! *Mon ami*, wait!" Dom panted and tripped abruptly on a branch in his path. He pitched sideways off the trail and screaming, fell over a small cliff. The decline was only about thirty feet in length, but he fell hard, hitting every bramble, bush, branch and stump on the way down.

At one point, his head hit something—either a stump or a rock so hard he saw stars, and lost consciousness as he came to a rolling stop under a boggy ledge, about forty-feet below where the cow moose now stood blowing and gazing about in confusion. Some two-legged creature had come too close to its calves and she was determined to stomp the interloper into the ground but… where did it go?

She bawled in frustration, dug furrows into the ground with her right front hoof, peered about once more, and finally turned around and ambled off.

Dom awoke under the root-filled ledge and heard a scramble above him. Cringing in fear he hunkered down with a hoarse shout and heard, "Dom! Where are you?"

"Bo! Oh, I thought you'd left me to die!" Dom exclaimed.

Bo, who had only prayed that he was far enough ahead of his friend that Dom would be killed instead of him, said, "No, not me! I would never leave you alone."

Dom stood up and both men peered about for the moose, while catching their breath. "That settles it," Bo said.

"What?" Dom asked.

"We have to find a town or some people," Bo replied. "We need food, and maybe some cash to survive." He hunkered down on one knee and fished around in his pocket for one of the maps he'd stolen from Bertrand's supplies. Tracing a grimy finger over a penciled in route, he said, "See? There is a town here, maybe thirty miles from where we stand. We have enough coin for victuals and a hotel room for a couple of nights. Maybe we could even sign on to another fur expedition…"

Dom frowned. "Why we do dat?" he murmured. "I thought you didn't want to work for no man?"

Bo shrugged. "I didn't know how hard it is to hunt and trap. Thought it was easy-peasy, but you see now how it is?" He held both hands out as if to present their barren landscape as a display. "The animals—they either run away or they turn and attack!"

Dom turned around and stared over his shoulder to where the crazed cow moose had disappeared. "*Oui*," he stated with disgust.

Bo put the map back in his pocket and pulled a

compass out. Watching as the gadget sought true north, he added, "Course, if we came upon some people by themselves, and they had what we seek, maybe we don't have to go all the way into a town—or, get a job."

Looking up at his much taller friend, Bo smiled slightly as a gleam entered Dom's eyes... the same gleam that had bonded their friendship so long ago in a different country and continent.

———

TWO DAYS LATER, and truly starving by now, Bo and Dom were belly crawling through bush, deadfall, pine needles and rich, loamy bark. Their focus was on a kid who was pulling a trap up from the ground by a small stream.

He was a good-looking teenage boy, except for a livid scar running across his right cheek. The boy was talking to himself and it sounded like he was quoting Bible passages.

In truth, Dan was learning how to read—per Jake's orders—and was using the Bible as a primer. Although he didn't much like learning about letters and arithmetic, Jake had insisted, and he had to admit that there was enough repetition within the endless Psalms to get a decent grasp on the written word.

Every night, after his chores were finished, and he and Jake sat down to dinner, he was expected to do some math problems and read two-three pages of the Bible to his foster-father. His devout murmurs now, were based less on true Christian beliefs and more on the fact that if he learned his sums and letters to Jake's satisfaction, he would be allowed to accompany the man into the town of Laramie come June 15th.

It was rumored that there would be a barter fair where they could sell their furs, and a gypsy carnival going on as well. Dan couldn't even imagine seeing so many people at once and the thought of a carnival (whatever that was), sounded like something he didn't want to miss.

These thoughts were running through his mind as he fetched his traps, removed their bounty, cleaned the metal contraptions and set them back up. He was concentrating so hard, he didn't notice the two wild-eyed, filthy French men that were advancing upon him with hunger in their eyes.

Bo and Dom couldn't help but notice the gun at the boy's hip or the fine shotgun that was propped up against a large boulder a few feet away from where he worked. Their attention was focused, instead, on the fat beaver the kid held in one hand… and the fact that he was, indeed, only a kid.

Bo pulled the pistol from his right pocket, aimed it at the boy and said, "Drop that animal on the ground, boy. Your guns too!"

Chapter Seventeen

JAKE, WHO WAS STANDING ABOUT 45-FEET AWAY, HEARD Bo's threatening hiss almost as soon as Dan did. Jake had always marveled at the echo quality surrounding this little area of the creek bed that looped around a copse of trees in a figure eight.

He and Dan had often carried on whole conversations while being out of sight of each other and Jake thanked his lucky stars now that he had heard the man's words even though the intruder obviously didn't know Jake was nearby.

Dropping down into a crouch, he pulled his .44 Navy Colt pistol and moved backwards so he could clap an eye on the situation. His heart was pounding slow and steady, even as his nerves drew taut with fear for the boy he had come to think of as a son.

For all the times he had cursed himself for becoming involved with the orphaned boy; all those times he'd had to decant his bottled-up emotions and let himself love again, for the frustration of having to teach the boy how to read and write, how to shoot, how to have good manners, how to be-essentially—the exact opposite of Jake, he knew without a shadow of a doubt, that he would die of grief if any harm came to the kid.

He crept through the underbrush as quietly as a ghost and ducking under the needled branches of a tamarack tree, he saw that two men were standing about 20-feet away from Dan. The boy was just now setting down the dead beaver with his left arm raised high in the air. Jake heard Dan say, "Whoa, mister... here's the animal, you can have him if you want!"

The smaller of the two men, a weaselly-faced varmint he could smell from 20-feet away, growled, "We'll take that, and any other meats you got stashed. First, though, you drop that gun and toss 'er over here."

Jake saw Dan hesitate for a moment, and prayed that the boy would do as ordered, despite the fact the he, himself, had instructed Dan to never surrender his gun in a fight. He could see that the much bigger man was holding a single-barreled shotgun on the boy and his index finger was twitching on the trigger.

He had figured to take the lead man out first as he seemed to be the catbird in charge, but the bigger man's itchy trigger hand was making Jake nervous. Dan had not yet handed over his gun, and the smaller man snarled, "Do it now, boy, afore I blast you to Kingdom Come!"

At which point, Jake fired a shot into the larger

man's back. Back shooting was not an honorable way to fight but Jake knew that "honor" had little to do with a bushwhack. All he wanted was for the big black mouth of that man's shotgun to stop pointing at his adopted son.

Jake got his wish but only just. Being shot tends to tighten people's muscles up and this time was no exception. Jake's shot sent Dom's hands straight up in the air, and his index finger squeezed the trigger on the shotgun. Black powder and pellets blasted the lower branches of the trees surrounding them, sending duff, pine needles, branches and cones to the ground.

The smaller man ducked and winced in shock as the shotgun's loud retort filled the air, but rage took over when he saw his friend fall like a downed ox. He pointed his pistol at the boy again and yelled over his shoulder, "Whoever ye are, you better put that gun down or the kid is dead!"

Bo was yelling over his shoulder at his invisible foe and trying to keep an eye on the boy too, which was hard right now as his whole back was tingling on high alert, waiting for the backstabbing metal that had just killed his closest friend to do the same thing to him.

He was so distracted by his own fear he didn't notice that Dan had dropped his left arm and taken ahold of his gun. One of the hardest things to learn during his shooting lessons was how to use both his hands in a gunfight. It was hard, and his left-hand felt like nothing more than a big, clumsy club when it came to pistol work, but Jake had insisted, and eventually, he'd learned.

Now, he was glad because the gnarly little man hadn't even noticed that he had another pistol on his left hip. He had started to carry guns on both hips because he never again wanted to be a helpless victim against an animal attack like he was six months' earlier. Although he never dreamed he'd be using his gun on a human being, the man seemed intent on killing him, so he pulled his left gun from its flat leather holster and shot him in the leg.

"Aiiieee!" Bo shouted and fell over backwards, clutching his right thigh in anguish. He turned his head and saw his friend Dom staring over at him with dead eyes. Turning back to Dan, he whimpered, "Hey... hey kid. Don't shoot me no more, okay?"

Dan was standing there, his mouth hanging open in shock at what he'd just done. But Jake stalked over, grabbed the pistol from Bo's hand and kicked the little French man in the ribs. Even as Bo shouted out in pain, Jake growled, "What d'ya think you're doing pulling a gun on a kid! You are trespassing on private property, and I have the right to shoot you dead!" He gave Bo another swift kick for emphasis.

"Owww!" Bo howled. "Please don't kick me no more—PLEASE!!"

Disgusted and infuriated, Jake walked over to where Dan stood trying—and failing—to place his still smoking pistol in his holster. Dan looked up and Jake could see that the youngster's eyes were red and spilling tears. "Don't weep over this piece of trash, kid. He was ready to drop you for one lousy beaver!"

More out of frustration than anything, Jake gave Dan's shoulders a little shake, which shook more tears from his eyes. Sighing, Jake took the boy by the arm, and led him over to a stump. "Sit down, Dan, and listen to me."

Dan sat and tried to wipe the moisture from his face. Then, he took hold of the canteen his foster father offered.

Jake sat across from him and both could hear the little French man weeping on the ground about twenty feet away.

Jake took a drink from his own canteen and spat on the ground. Looking at Dan, he said, "Shooting a man is the last thing any 'good' man wants to do, and I appreciate that you have strong feelings about what just happened. Shows me that you are—or will be—a 'good' man.

"But not all men are good, see? This man here not only wanted your food, he was willing to shoot you dead to take your food and everything else you owned! Trash like that ain't worth your tears!"

Jake stared hard at Dan and continued. "Now, go on back to the house and clean yourself up. Chickens need to be fed, and you can bring out some o' that honey we found a couple of days ago for our supper."

He stood up and watched as Dan walked slowly back to the house. Then he turned around, rolled up his sleeves and went to work.

The chickens had just run up to Dan, chuckling and eager for their daily grain, when he heard the loud report of Jake's gun. He turned around and gazed at the far side of the pasture but couldn't see or hear anything unusual... only the crickets and meadowlarks filling their small valley with their daily refrain.

Chapter Eighteen

1879

THE SECOND WEEKEND of June 1879 rolled around, finally, and Dan was as excited as a newborn calf. Jake had pulled their old wagon around the front of the house and they spent the early morning hours filling it with trade-goods. There were furs, pelts, leather goods, apples, small kegs of bear fat and eggs in crates and boxes. Satisfied, Jake figured they had enough supplies on hand to barter for the things they'd grown short on like metal, medicine, cloth and new cookware.

The weather was warm and balmy, and they set out from the farm about 9:00 a.m. As they traveled through the green valleys, Dan felt the shrouds of depression and remorse lifting from his heart. He knew that those two, dead strangers had meant him and Jake harm and if left unchecked, they would have killed them both and stolen from them everything they owned.

Still, their deaths had weighed heavy on his mind and often, over the last couple of months, he had woken up in the night with a shout of fright at the nightmares that haunted his sleep.

He was upset that Jake had killed the man that he had simply shot in the leg. "Why did you have to kill him, sir? He was already wounded and disarmed…"

At first, Jake refused to answer Dan's questions, but finally he said, "What was I supposed to do, huh?" Jake glared at Dan who was preparing breakfast. "Just set him up on his horse, and say, 'Giddyap?'"

Dan had shrugged but his attitude was plain and filled with horror and disapproval. Jake barked, "Don't you shrug your shoulders at me, kid! You got some-thing to say, you turn around and face me like a man!"

Dan set down his spoon and turned to face his foster father. "Yeah, that's what you shoulda done, sir, but instead, you killed him and buried him, without a by-your-leave! It was wrong… Sir!"

Jake had stared Dan down, but his face was red, and his chest heaved with emotion. He pinned his foster son with wild eyes for a moment, and Dan had wondered if he'd gone too far in his critical assessment of Jake's actions. Then, Jake sat down at the table with a sigh. "Sit down, Dan."

Dan hesitated, and Jake said something so rare, it struck an awful fear in his heart.

"Please, son. Sit down."

Jake continued once Dan had taken a seat. "There was no good way out of that situation, see. I had already killed the man's friend, so he woulda come back for revenge, if nothing else. Or—he would have holed-up and sniped at us from the tree line once he was healed. Even worse, he mighta headed into town and told the local law about what happened."

He stared into Dan's eyes and said, "I ain't no kind of friend to the law, Dan. I got some pretty bad things on my sheet, and I figure as long as I leave them law-dogs alone, they'll return the favor. But, if they catch wind of me, they'll follow through—and that would be the end—for both of us."

Jake studied Dan's face and he could see curious thoughts running through his eyes like panicked rabbits. "No," he sighed. "I ain't about to share my... checkered past with you, so forget about your questions, okay?"

Dan nodded, but seemed dissatisfied with Jake's response. A loaded silence filled the room as Dan played with his food and Jake brooded, but finally, the older man said, "I atoned, Dan. I've done my level best to atone for all I done wrong. Think what you want about what I done to those two drifters, I don't care. Just know this... I have been around men like that most of my life, and they were no good!" Jake heaved a great sigh. "Trust me—it takes one to know one."

Suddenly, the fear and resentment in Dan's heart melted away. Looking up at his mentor and seeing the weight of the years pressing down on Jake's face and his lean frame, Dan had to admit that he had always known Jake was some sort of outlaw, or at least, he *had* been before Dan came along.

It had been almost five years since the day Jake had found and rescued him from those bad bandits and since then, Dan knew the man had done his very best to make life as good as possible for him. He was tough, but never mean. He was patient, and generous with what knowledge he had. He was a good mentor, and Dan loved him.

Heart filled with gratitude, and barely understood pity, Dan suddenly stood up, crossed to Jake's side of the table and gave the man a rare, awkward hug. "Thank you, sir. I... I love you, Jake," he whispered.

Touched, Jake reached his arms up to hug him back.

Bernard Achilles and Dominique Etienne were never referred to again.

———

NOW, the sun smiled down on them like a benevolent uncle as they made their way into the town of Laramie. It had taken about two days to get there, and Dan was practically squirming with excitement as they drew near. Both could see numerous plumes of smoke rising from the other end of town and knew just where to go for the action.

Dan kept sneaking a peek at his foster-father who was, by now, almost unrecognizable from the man he usually lived with. Jake had taken a long bath in a creek earlier that morning and taken the time to cut his hair and shave his beard and mustache off. He wore his best duds now—a gray suit, an elaborately embroidered vest, snowy white shirt, and black dress boots.

He looked much thinner than usual though, almost gaunt, and Dan wondered if the man was getting enough to eat. But still, he was struck by how handsome Jake was, when he took the time to groom-up.

Dan had smiled when Jake approached looking as fresh and shiny as a new penny and said, "You look real nice, sir."

Jake grinned in reply and answered, "You might look to yerself, Dan. You're looking like a ragamuffin'. Here's some soap..."

Dan rolled his eyes and sighed but did as ordered and scrubbed his body until his skin squeaked. He was shocked when he walked, dripping, back to their small camp and saw a new pair of canvas pants, a new shirt and a pair of shiny leather boots laid out for him on the wagon's tailgate. "Where did these come from?" he asked.

Jake shrugged, "Put in an order on the sly, last time Ol' Chew came through. Yer growing like a weed, and I thought you'd want to look fine for all the young ladies coming for the carnival."

Dan was doubtful that new clothes would hide his facial scar but was grateful, nevertheless, for the new duds. Feeling like a million bucks, he strutted around the wagon like a cock rooster, until Jake blew a raspberry at him and said, "Load up before you make me sick and I have to turn this wagon around and go back home!"

They made their way down Main Street, and even before they saw the gigantic encampment spread out before them in the valley beyond the city's boundaries, they heard the dull roar of a crowd, chanting and Indian drums.

Dan gazed up at Jake in joy and the older man felt a knife enter his heart. The kid would be wanting to go out and see the world soon. That was the way of young men. He only hoped that he would have time to teach Dan everything he could think about survival before the boy left for good.

Chapter Nineteen

Jake drew the wagon up to a cluster of tents, tables, racks and small bonfires. He stopped the horses and fished around in his pant's pocket for a moment. Then he said, "Here ya go. Buy yourself something you like." He held a five-dollar coin in his hand.

Dan stared at the cash money and said, "Me? I can have all that?" He'd never seen so much money in his life and to have it handed to him seemed too good to be true.

Jake nodded and gave out a small smile. "It ain't all that much, kid, but it's yours. Now..." he frowned slightly. "There's a lot of good stuff to look at, but you'd better be careful. Don't go near the fighting pens, there's a lot of bad men around there who like to take advantage of folks', especially youngsters."

He stared about for a couple more seconds and said, "Also, don't get lured into the gypsy's camp. I like those folks well enough, but they'll steal anything that ain't nailed down. Got it?"

Dan nodded, and said, "No fighting pens and no gypsies, sir."

Jake continued. "I'll do the trading today and it'll take a few hours, so come back to the wagon at about sunset… that would be five or six hours—about 7:30. Don't make me come lookin' for ya, okay?

Dan grinned and agreed. "Yes, sir! I'll be back at sunset, promise!"

During the short time they'd talked, more wagons had pulled up next to them and people were unloading their goods for trade. Dan said, "Goodbye!" and took off in the direction of a large crowd that was whoopin' and hollering in the distance. He could see plumes of dust rising in the air and heard frantic hoof beats.

Coming closer he saw that, of all things, a donkey race was going on. Colorfully—dressed children were perched on the donkey's backs, urging their mounts with loud cries and the liberal use of some sort of soft, cloth quirts. The braided quirts had bells sewn on the ends and made quite a racket as the kids smacked their mounts on the rump and shook the noisy quirts over their ears.

One boy clearly held the lead. He looked to be in his middle teens, about Dan's age, but he was small and wiry, with wildly curling black hair. Often, he would stop his donkey well ahead of the other kids, shake his fist in the air, laugh and yell indecipherable obscenities at them.

Dan stayed and watched for a few minutes, grinning with amusement and admiration as the races continued. The kids went from donkeys-to mules, and finally, to horses and the wild-haired boy won every match. Finally, the races were over, and Dan saw an equally wild-haired man, standing in front of the crowd collecting the boy's cash winnings.

Dan wandered away then and walked over to a set of long booths and tables. He passed a cock fight and, indeed, saw an unsavory crowd gathered around cheering and cursing the bloody, mad-eyed roosters. Further on, he saw another fight being bet on, but these were dogs.

Snarls and anguished cries filled the air and Dan hurried by and tried not to look. Finally, he saw a booth surrounded by hungry people and smelled something wonderful. Wandering closer, he saw two little boys sitting close to a stump and eating something brown and shiny.

He gazed down at their happy, sticky faces and asked, "Whatcha got there?"

"Caramel apple!" one of the boy's managed through a mouthful of sweets.

Dan fingered the five-dollar coin in his pocket and stepped into line in front of the booth. Apparently, caramel was on the menu; he saw caramel popcorn, nuts, apples and apple/caramel cakes for sale. He stepped up to a plump, pink-cheeked lady behind the counter, placed his coin on the bar and said, "One caramel apple, please."

"Coming right up!" she grinned and moved away to fetch an apple, poke a stick into it and plunge it into a vat of warm caramel. She brought the candied apple back to him, took his coin and was honest with the change, although she tried to tempt the rest of the change back in exchange for more caramel treats.

He shook his head no, though, and wandered off to take in the sights while eating the apple and trying to keep the candy coating off his new clothes. Messy as his snack was, it was indescribably delicious.

Finally, he heard the haunting sound of guitar strings rising through the rough, American landscape like warm smoke through cold water. He also felt a hush from the watching crowd of people interspersed with occasional cat-calls and low whistles. He wormed his way to the front of the crowd and stood, staring in shock at the most beautiful vision his eyes had ever beheld.

Two women were dancing for the crowd. Well... one woman and one girl, maybe Dan's age, were dancing to the exotic melody. They wore colorful clothes that seemed to be made of nothing but silk scarves, the ends of which fluttered enticingly with every move they made. They moved slowly, at first, taking long, dipping steps in rhythm with the stringed instrument.

Their movements were so sinuous, so... desirous, Dan felt a stirring akin to his most shameful moments —always before felt only in privacy and to be avoided if possible. Looking around, however, he was obviously not the only male who was getting stirred up by the gorgeous female dancers.

Suddenly, small round wooden clackers appeared in the females' hands and the guitar rhythms picked up speed. As the guitarist beat a tattoo on the wooden face of his instrument, and the women threw their arms and hands skyward, the audience spontaneously broke into their own clapping, keeping time with the dance.

Even Dan started clapping time and let out a shout of approval as the women dipped and swirled and twirled to the beat. Then, it was over, and the female's disappeared into the crowd on onlookers, as more money exchanged hands.

Dan shook his head and grinned. He knew he would never forget the gypsy women and how their dancing had lifted his heart and soul.

———

HEART STILL BEATING with the sound of Spanish guitar music, Dan wandered on taking in the sights. There were so many new and interesting things to look at, he wasn't sure where to begin finding a gift for his foster father. Then, he came upon a leather goods booth, and stopped to gaze at the fine leatherwork. There were saddles, braided reins, bridles, boots, belts, hatbands, sheaths and several more items decorating his long table. Each piece was a work of art.

An old man behind the table stared at him as Dan

gazed at the displays and asked, "Whatcher lookin' fer, boy?"

Dan blushed and fingered the $4.95 in his pants pocket. Smiling, he answered, "Well, I was looking for a present for my dad, but I guess I don't have enough cash to buy here... everything is very beautiful, sir. Did you make all this stuff?"

The man grinned, showing toothless gums, and answered, "Aye, I did. Learnt leather work when I was just a sprout—my own daddy taught me—God rest him."

Dan nodded. "I see nothing here is priced... can I ask how much that sheath is?" He pointed at one of the plainer knife sheaths.

The oldster studied Dan's face and said, "My name is Jerome Smalley—what's yours?"

Dan's eyes grew wide, and he stammered, thinking he'd been rude not to introduce himself. "Oh, my name is Daniel Monroe—sorry. Pleased to make your acquaintance." He held out a hand to shake, as he'd been taught to do when he was just small.

Smalley grinned. He'd already decided he liked this kid and was touched that the boy clearly wanted to give his old man a gift. His leather goods usually cost a pretty penny, but occasionally, he was moved to give his items away for free. He had no family of his own— not anymore—and no one to leave his custom to, so the rare charity hurt no one and sometimes filled his old heart with joy.

"Wahl, I don't usually ask a customer for their

name, nor do I volunteer mine, but I figure a friend is a different story. Don't you agree?"

Dan smiled in return. "Yessir... friends oughta know each other's names."

Turning away, Smalley shuffled slowly to a large trunk. He opened it up and fished around for a few moments. Then he found what he'd been looking for. Holding it up, he studied it fondly for a few moments and then turned back to the long table. "How do you like this one, Daniel Monroe?"

Dan's eyes grew wide as he studied the elaborate sheath. It was made of two different leathers—the backing dark, and the front piece much lighter. Somehow, the man had been able to cut intricate scrollwork into the lighter leather and die the cut-outs with red, green, blue and purple dyes. There were two small Conchos punched into the belt loop which seemed to reflect the sheaths dyes in the bright afternoon sun.

It was one of the most beautiful things he'd ever seen, and his mouth watered. He could only imagine the look in Jake's eyes as he received this gift. But imagining was about the best he could do... one look at that beautiful piece and he knew it was far too expensive for the likes of him.

"Oh, sir. It's one of the prettiest things I've ever seen —for sure."

Smalley grinned. "Wahl, it's yourn for one dollar... and two or three wagons of wood for my fire. Deal?"

Dan's mouth hung open for a second, and then he gasped in delight. "Oh sir, do you mean it—really?"

The old man was tickled. This kid had made his day. "Oh, I'm sure alright. Just don't go lettin' on that I strike a good deal oncet a while—I gotta reputation to maintain."

"Yes, sir!" Dan agreed and fished a dollars' worth of change out of his pocket. Then he asked, "Sir, do you know where I can find some wood for your fire?" He gazed around at the crowd that stood three people deep in places.

Smalley said, "Yup. Go thata way, about a quarter mile. There are a bunch of fallen trees just within the tree-line. You can take my push-barrow and fill it up a coupla times. Then, we'll be even, and you can give yer pa a gift he won't never forget."

"Yes, sir—right away, Mr. Smalley, and thanks!" Dan headed toward an old, wooden cart with two handles and a large metal wheel in front, picked it up and started heading east toward a wooded hillside. He found the deadfall right away and loaded the wagon up with as much wood as he could lift. Then he pushed the barrow back and, weaving cautiously through the crowds of people, deposited the wood next to Smalley's little booth.

The oldster smiled, stood up, offered Dan a ladle of water from his keg and said, "One more load, and we got us a deal!"

Dan nodded and said, "Be right back, Mr. Smalley!" Turning the cumbersome wagon around, he headed back to the wood pile, but he was a little past half way there when a commotion to his right caught his attention.

A ring of young men stood in a circle around something on the ground. One man stood close to a wriggling, squirming burlap sack, and delivered it a kick as Dan watched. "Give it over, Gyp, or we'll kill ya, you hear me?"

Dan was too far away to hear what the squeaking, snarling sack said in return, but he thought he recognized the gypsy boy's curses—only now his strident voice was muffled with tears and pain. Again, the cowboy-looking fellow hollered, "I done told ya—give over those winnin's or my buddies and me will kill ya!"

Dan saw that there were four men beating up and trying to rob the much younger and smaller gypsy teenager, and he sighed. Jake had taught him that a good man should always try his best to keep the innocent from suffering at the hands of bullies.

Pulling his guns from both holsters, he shouted, "Hold up there, and stop tormenting that kid, or I'll shoot!"

Chapter Twenty

JAKE HAD GOTTEN A GOOD DEAL ON ALL HIS TRADE goods and he was pleased. He now owned a new set of cookware, some decent forks and spoons, two small cutting knives, a wagonload of oats and four large barrels of feed corn for the livestock. He had also run into a well-known dentist and purchased something called heroin—a mixture of opium and alcohol made by some fancy-pants medicine patent company that guaranteed a cessation of pain with regular use.

Lately, he had a fierce ache in his lower left side—sometimes in his belly and other times wrapping around his ribs and lower back. He also felt kinda light-headed on occasion, and tired easily. He didn't know what was wrong, and didn't much care either, but there were always chores to do around the ranch, and he wasn't finished teaching Dan what he needed to know to get along in life. A little sip of medicine here and there wouldn't hurt and would keep him going strong for a while.

Still, after spending the last four hours trading, lifting, and hauling goods back and forth from his wagon, he was tuckered. He made his way through the trading area and saw a small grove of Aspens by a creek. He saw a few other families tucked in amongst the trees, eating and relaxing in the shade, and figured he'd join them for the next couple of hours while his foster son got some socializing out of his system.

Sitting down on a fallen log with a groan, Jake looked through the trees and realized he could see a lot of the "fair" area from where he sat. He heard some fiddle music and saw the back of a few trading tents. He also noticed four brightly colored wagons pulled up in a circle. He recognized them as "gypsy" wagons; the prairie schooners were painted in garish hues and the canvas tarps covering them sported strange, mystical symbols like huge elongated eyeballs, tattooed hands, golden crowns and black gallows.

He shook his head with a grin. He'd met quite a few Romany folks over the years and found them to be a likeable bunch, but most of them were about as mystical as Dan's pet goat. Still, a few of the older gypsy grannies believed in the old ways, and there were plenty of suckers out here in the American west looking for an edge to their mostly hard-scrabble existence; like having their futures read or buying some sort of "Love Potion" to ensure finding a good mate or even purchasing a magical token to keep an eminent Indian attack from ever happening.

Suddenly, he saw a flurry of activity close to the gypsies' encampment. Focusing his eyes, he gazed across a meadow and saw four cowboys hauling a twitching, squirming sack between them. Jake realized the men had either caught an animal or a person and he watched the action with interest.

The men walked about fifty-feet closer to where Jake sat and dumped the sack on the ground. Then, one of the men started kicking the bag and Jake heard a painful howl issue forth. "Damn..." he muttered softly and frowned. Whatever or whomever those men were tormenting was much smaller than the smallest of them, and dangerously vulnerable.

He hated seeing this sort of thing happen—he'd seen the strong torment the weak too often in his life. He remembered recently teaching Dan to never be a bully and not to tolerate that kind of behavior in others. Still, Jake needed to keep a low profile right now, and knew he couldn't get involved in such a public display so he decided to ignore the scene and take a small nap. He tipped his hat down over his eyes and pretended he didn't hear the anguished cries coming from the sack.

He was so tired, he almost fell asleep despite the racket, until a familiar voice rang out in the late, after-noon air. "Hold up there, and stop tormenting that kid, or I'll shoot!"

Jake eyes flew open and he cringed. *Damn!*, he

thought. There was his own foster son now, challenging a pack of bullies, and Jake couldn't take Dan to task over it, since he-himself had just drilled that lesson into the kid's head. Jake reached over to where his long rifle was strapped to his rucksack, grabbed it, sat up on one knee and rested his gun on a tree trunk. Looking through the sight, he took careful study of the situation.

Dan was standing some forty-feet away from the cowboys, holding both his pistols at the ready. Dan looked dead-serious, For the most part, the men were standing silent, in a state of surprised shock, but one of the men—a burly fellow with a black eye-patch who seemed older than his friends—took a slow step backward, so he was out of the line of fire. He was also pulling open the flap on his widow maker holster, so he could grab ahold of his pistol.

Jake sighed—that man would be the first to go. The scene in front of him seemed to come to a stand-still, except for the frantic grunts of the cowboys' prisoner, who had found the sacks opening and was squirming through it as fast as he could go. A dark—haired boy burst through the sack, ran about thirty-feet toward the gypsy camp and then stopped, turned around and made an obscene gesture involving his right arm and a raised middle finger. Then, he skedaddled out of sight.

A few tense moments passed as the cowboys appraised the situation, and Jake's trigger finger tightened. Then two deputies sauntered up, grinning. "Jackson, looks like you got a live one here... we oughta just let this boy have his way with you and your high jinks." The taller of the two lawmen called out.

"Aw, shucks, Deputy, this sprout was just fixin' to clean his barrels out, that's all. Probly woulda shot his own foot off!" The kick-happy cowboy responded, and the scene suddenly dissolved into laughter.

Jake saw one of the deputies talking to Dan; who put his guns away, shrugged, picked up a push-barrow and started walking toward the trees ringing the pasture. He couldn't help but wonder what the boy was up to.

The other deputy walked over to the cowboys and told them to scram and stop harassing folks. Those boys were apparently well-known as "trouble-makers" by the local law dogs. As they walked off, he heard the men talking about stupid, sassy kids who thought they were "Gun Hands," and how *they* would have made short work of the kid and his threats.

Jake couldn't help but grin, though, and shake his head. He had no doubt that at least three of those men would have found themselves whistling Dixie at the Pearly Gates before they even knew what had hit them.

The other man with the eager pistol might have proven a problem for Dan, but Jake shrugged. That's why he was here, right? To watch the boy's back.

Chapter Twenty-One

AFTER DAN FOUND JAKE, THEY HEADED FOR HOME. IT would take them a day and a half to arrive, but Jake was eager to leave society behind and get back to his beloved valley. Dan said nothing about the altercation, and since Jake had taken a hearty sip of his new medicine, he was content to let his pain fade and relax against the wagon's backboard as the horses picked their way through the valley.

Jake dozed off and Dan stared in surprise when he saw the horse's leads go slack in Jake's hands. He worked the leather through Jake's numb fingers, gave the reins a twitch and settled in for another hours' ride to the foothills. Glancing over at Jake, he wondered why his adopted 'Pa' was so tired. *Oh well, he's pretty old,* he thought, trying to figure Jake's age. He couldn't exactly recall, but he thought Jake was about forty-years-old... or thereabouts.

He gazed around, as always, vigilant against hostiles —Indian or otherwise, but could see nothing for miles. The sun had gone behind the mountains by now, but it's lasting shadow cast the valley in a bluish light which seemed to bring every tree, shrub, and rock into stark relief.

Staring ahead, Dan recognized their campsite from the night before and made for that direction. Pulling up to the smoke darkened ring of rocks around their recent cook fire, he jumped down, loosened the horses from the traces and led them toward a small stream. Then he hobbled them and brought each a nose sack of grain.

Walking back, he saw that Jake was still asleep. He frowned, wondering if he should worry, but jumped up and shook the man's left arm. "Jake... wake up! We're here."

Jake started and stared about, blinking like an owl. "Oh... hmmm," he muttered. He shook his head and whispered, "Must have dropped off..."

Then he climbed down off the wagon and helped Dan bring some meat and biscuits out of the back of the wagon for their dinner. They had just sat down to drink some coffee and wait for their dinner to heat when Dan smiled, and headed back to the wagon. Walking back, he held out the beautiful leather knife sheath. "Here you go, sir. I bought this for you."

Jake's eyes got big as he studied the hand-tooled sheath. It was very, very nice and would have cost two-three times what Dan possessed in cash. "This is pretty as a picture, son, but... how did you buy it?"

Dan grinned, "Well, I didn't steal it, if that's what you mean. I handed over a dollar and fetched the seller three loads of firewood. That's how I could get it for ya. Do you like it?"

Remembering the boy and his push-barrow, sudden tears moistened Jake's eyes, and he swiped at his face with mortified embarrassment. He never cried—not ever—and now his emotions were runnin' away from him over one simple act of kindness. "I... I love it, Dan. This is the nicest thing I've ever owned. Thank you."

Dan stirred the coals in the fire and let his foster father collect himself. He was grinning inside, though, and proud of himself for giving Jake such a fine gift.

Jake stared at the sheath for a few moments and then said, "That was foolish what you done, Dan. You know that, right?"

Dan blushed. He had no idea that Jake had, somehow, found out about his challenge to those no-goods. He had known that it was four against one—which were obviously bad odds, but he had confidence in his gun skills and had thought that he was doing the right thing—at least at that moment.

Over the last few hours, though, as he'd driven the horses to their campsite, he'd wondered about his compulsion to try and save that kid from those bullies. If things had gone sideways—even a little bit, Jake might be standing over his cold dead body right now, instead of cooking meat on a warm, starry evening.

Dan ducked his head. "Sir, I didn't know you'd heard about that. I'm sorry, it was probably pretty stupid, but I couldn't stand what those men were doing to that poor kid. They were trying to rob him of his winnings, and I saw that kid race. He won every one of those races fair and square! It wasn't fair, and then, when that one man started kicking the kid, something inside me just snapped. They were wrong to do that!"

Jake sighed. "I know. They were wrong to do what they done, but you gotta know when to act and when to walk away, see? The odds were against you from the get-go."

"How'd you find out about it, sir?" Dan asked.

Jake grinned. "Believe it or not, I was watchin' the whole time. It was kinda a fluke, really, but I had my sight set one the one big cowboy in back of the bunch. He was your only threat, but I had your back. He wasn't gonna to get the drop on you."

Dan's eyes gleamed in the firelight. "Thank you, sir. I appreciate that."

Jake nodded, but added, "Do I have your word that you won't step into any more foolishness without considering things first? Consider the odds—the logistics, how many enemies you're facing, and how many bullets you need to fight them off. Using your brains instead of your guns sometimes will mean the difference between life and death. Understood?"

Dan nodded, "Yes sir, I understand—and, I promise."

"Okay, 'nuff said," Jake answered. "Now, let's get some shut-eye. I wanna take off at first light."

"Okay, sir, good night, sir."

Jake held on to that sheath for the rest of the evening, turning it this way and that as the fire's flames caught the tiny Conchos and reflected the colored leather into his sparkling, dazzled eyes.

Chapter Twenty-Two

THEY MADE THEIR WAY BACK HOME, AND FOR A WHILE things went back to normal. Jake seemed to feel better, and there was often a twinkle in his eye as he joined Dan in their daily chores, like weeding the corn patch, fixing fencing and bringing in enough wood to keep warm over the coming winter.

One day, Dan stood up from where he was kneeling in the garden and saw two wagons approaching. Shading his eyes from the fierce overhead sun, he peered through the lazy dust clouds and saw the old tinker, Boss Chew, driving his wagon up to the house. Another wagon followed, one Dan did not recognize.

Jake, however, did recognize the wagon and the tiny man perched on the driver's bench. His name was Archie Banyon and he was one of the best tutors in the territory. Although he had decided not to make too much of a fuss over Dan's hasty actions at the barter fair, Jake realized the boy needed more education and a better understanding of the world around him, if he were to survive on his own.

Sure, Dan knew his letters, and a little mathematics and how to use a gun and a knife, but he didn't have any practical experience with people and how to walk among them. Usually, good parents could instill a moral code into their child and if he had the time, he would do just that. But, after a long talk with the town doctor, Jake knew his time on Earth was winding down.

So, as soon as he'd gotten home, he sent a message on, asking if Archie was available to educate his boy. The answer to that question was, apparently, yes, and Jake grinned in satisfaction. The only rub was that Archie would need to live with them here, as Jake could not risk exposing Dan to the citizens of Laramie—especially those who worked in cahoots with Heck Giddings.

Gazing up at Archie's Prairie Schooner-style wagon, Jake saw it was stuffed to the rafters with supplies, and he knew the tutor was here to stay. "Howdy!" he called up to Archie who gazed down at him with happy eyes.

"Hello… you are Mr. Conrad, yes?" Archie replied, and then glancing toward Dan, added, "And… you must be my student?"

Dan's jaw dropped, and he said, "Um, well, my name's Daniel Munroe, anyway. Pleased to make your acquaintance."

Archie, understanding abruptly that the boy wasn't

at all aware of what was going on grinned and climbed down off his wagon. Dan was shocked at the man's diminutive size. Although he was perfectly formed, he stood no more than five-feet-tall, as if he was a child playing grown-up. His hair was gray, though and he sported deep crow's feet at the corners of his jolly brown eyes.

Jake had wandered off to greet old Boss and lead his horse to the water trough, and Archie knew that it was up to him to make the boy understand he was his new teacher. Luckily, the kid had good manners, and although he was clearly at a loss for words, he asked, "Shall we bring your hoss over to the trough, sir? Bet he's thirsty in this heat."

"Yes, let's do that," Archie agreed and as they led the horse to the trough, he said, "Your father has hired me to be your tutor, Dan. I hope you don't mind?"

Dan stopped walking and stared over his shoulder to where Jake was leaning over Boss' wares as if nothing out of the ordinary was happening. He frowned in exasperation. *Ain't it just like Jake to spring something like this on me without even a by yer leave!* he thought.

Still, his good manners took over, and he said, "Sir, do you mind if I go have a word with my pa? There's a ladle, right there, if'n you need a drink for yourself." Then he strode off to where Jake stood by Boss' wagon, sipping from a fresh bottle of newly-purchased whiskey.

Archie dipped his head, hiding his grin. He would

be staying on for however long it took to give this boy a good education—he had already been paid for his services. Happily, for him anyway, Dan seemed to be a good kid, polite and for the most part, well-spoken. He would not be hard to teach.

Meanwhile, Dan asked to speak to Jake—in private—and Jake followed his boy up onto the porch and into the house. Dan, who was angrier at being tricked than he was at having a teacher thrust upon him for no good reason, said, "Jake! What's going on? I already know my letters and even some multiples and such! Why'd you go and hire a tutor for me?"

Jake shrugged and answered, "You done it to yerself, Dan. Once you pulled your guns on those men at the barter fair, I knew that you had no more sense than a chicken in a rain storm! I never got after you for what you done, but I knew you needed the kind of education, I don't know how to give. That's what Archie will do fer you, and I won't hear no sass from you over it, either."

Thus informed, Dan shrugged and sat down at the table. "Coulda filled me in, sir. I mean, I knew I got off easy, but now I feel like a fool!"

"What you did *was* foolish, Dan. Well-meant but foolish. Archie… and that's *Mr. Banyon* to you, son, is one of the best teachers around and he's going to give you a decent education. And, you're going to be a better than decent student. Are we clear?"

Dan's shoulders dropped, and he sighed long and

loud until Jake began to glare. Then he said, "Yes, sir. We're clear."

———

TWO WEEKS LATER, Jake, Dan and Archie received visitors. It was early in the morning and Dan was fetching firewood for the cook stove. Jake had stepped outside to relieve himself when they both heard soft music tinkling through the misty dawning. Looking out over the valley, they saw four wagons down by the creek, and both immediately recognized the gaily painted tarps and garish paint jobs adorning the gypsy's train.

Looking closer, Dan saw a masculine figure wave at them, and Jake said, "Wahl, looks like your gypsy friends have come to say hello."

Dan grinned and said, "I never met none of them, sir, but they sure do know how to ride... and dance!"

Jake grinned. "Clapped your eyes on their women-folk, eh?"

Dan glanced down and murmured. "'Twern't intentional, sir. They were just there, dancing away and they were so... so beautiful."

Jake nodded. "Those folks are Romany, I reckon. A lot of them come from eastern Europe, like Arabia and Russia, but some of them come from Spain... I think these folks may be of that variety."

How do you figure, sir?"

"I heard their music at the fair... that was Spanish music. I think it's called flamenco or some such." He scratched his head and said, "Guess we better walk on down there and see if they're just passing through or if they need some help."

They walked across the pasture that was filled with dew-laden wildflowers, and as they approached the gypsies' camp many of the inhabitants gathered together and started clapping their hands together and cheering in approval.

Dan almost turned around to see what was causing their visitors to react in such a manner, but he knew there was no one behind them and that the gypsies must have seen what he'd done to protect one of their own.

His cheeks heated up and got even hotter when Jake cuffed him on the shoulder and said, "A hero is born, Dan boy! Just don't let it go to your head, alright?"

Dan murmured, "Yes, Sir!"

So, they approached their visitors amidst the sound of clapping hands, fiddles, a guitar and another stringed instrument, Jake later identified as a mandolin.

The wild-haired boy stood alongside an older man, and it didn't take a genius to figure out they were father and son. The little man with curly black hair, a bright red bandana, leather vest, multi-colored velvet belt, and numerous pieces of jewelry stepped up with his hand extended. "*Hola*," he said with a wide smile. "My name is Pedro Amaya. Please, pardon the intrusion but my son—my little Manny, wanted to say *gracias*...um, thank you to the brave boy who saved his life."

Jake smirked, but his big hand nudged Dan forward so he faced the boy, who looked to be about Dan's age, but much smaller. The boy seemed almost as embarrassed as Dan, but he stepped up, grinned and held out his hand to shake. "Yes, my name is Manuel, and it was me you saved from those bad men. I wanted to say thank you and tell you I'm in your debt now and forever—or until I am able to return the favor."

Dan ducked his head. "Well, I didn't actually do anything, so you don't owe me any favors, okay?"

The boy shook his head. "Oh no, compadre. I do, and don't you worry... if you ever need help, me Manuel Amaya, will be there by your side."

Liking the boy immediately—his bright brown eyes, his merry smile and the fervor of his promises, Dan said, "Well, okay then. That's great—thanks!"

The smell of good food cooking wafted through the air and Pedro, who seemed to be the leader (or Rom) of this caravan said, "Come! We have made a feast for you and your fine, brave son. Please, take your repast, and then we will be on our way, *si*?"

Jake, who had been eating little the last few weeks, suddenly felt his stomach growl like a crotchety old bear. He smiled, said, "Gracias," and walked toward the gypsies' cook fire where venison was roasting over hot coals, and several hot side dishes were set out on a long table. Dan went to fetch Archie, who was reading a book down by the creek and soon the three of them were treated to a wonderful Romany feast.

He knew a smattering of Spanish and as he filled his belly, he listened to the gypsies as they talked, laughed, and praised the prowess of his foster son, who didn't understand a word they were saying but knew they were talking about him so, he simply squirmed in embarrassment.

It was a good visit and informative. The gypsies were anxious to take their leave but explained their origins as best they knew how. Their band had been traveling the cross roads of America for two generations, but their forefathers were originally from Northern Spain and were known as Andalusians.

They were apparently a happy, peaceful bunch and friends to one and all—white men and Indians alike. They were on their way to the Idaho Territory to reunite with their extended family and anxious to arrive before the snows fell. Still, they felt they must stop and pay homage to the boy who had not only saved the leader's son but had managed to keep intact the cash money the gypsies had earned from the fair.

Then they presented gifts to Dan for his bravery and to Jake for raising such a fine boy. Dan received one of the silken quirts the Roms used to train even the wildest of horses to a state of calm obedience. He was also given a lovely leather coat with colorful designs on the back, fringes and a stand-up, fur collar.

Jake received two beautiful table coverings, and a packet of herbal medicine. The old granny, or Wise

Woman of the band had taken one look at Jake and fetched the small leather sack from her wagon. She pressed it into his hands with a shy grunt. "You take a pinch in your morning coffee," she murmured.

Jake gazed at the concoction and nodded in thanks.

Then, they were gone. But the last thing young Manny said as they rolled off into the distance was, "You need me, you come and find me, sí? A place called Boise, Idaho Territory. Promise!"

Dan yelled back, "Yes, thank you... I will, I promise!"

Chapter Twenty-Three

SEVEN MONTHS LATER, AS THE FIRST BLUEBELLS WERE beginning to dot the upper slopes of the valley, Jake and Dan received more company. Again, they were taken by surprise, and Jake frowned uneasily. He was slipping in his constant vigilance against his enemies. Sleeping far too often, and much too heavily, he had dropped his guard, and he knew that if he wasn't careful, Dan would bear the brunt of Jake's recklessness.

He and Dan had woken up and stepped outside to pee when they heard a dog barking, and saw the tall, pointed poles of five tipis set up across the meadow in the shade of a grove of beech and aspen trees. Jake relaxed immediately; he recognized the tipis as belonging to his dead wife's people.

He and Dan had wondered the last couple of years what had become of their friends... the band usually stopped by once a year on their way either north, for the buffalo, or south to escape the harsh Wyoming winters. But Iron Kettle's people had stopped coming in the spring of 1876.

Jake worried that they may have become caught up in the Greasy Grass War, which had finally brought Custer and many of his soldiers' lives to a violent end. Jake had heard that Sitting Bull and his consolidated tribes considered Custer's defeat a great triumph for the Indian nations, but the backlash of their victory was swift and terrible.

Since the Battle of the Little Big Horn, the U.S. army had systematically hunted down the participating tribes and slaughtered them—wholesale. Six years earlier, Iron Kettle had boasted over forty tipis, and now Jake could see only five. This tribe had suffered great loss.

"Look, Jake!" Dan exclaimed with a smile. "It's Iron Horse and his people!"

Jake nodded. "Yup, but things don't look so good for them. Let's go down and see what's happened."

Dan grabbed their new coffeepot, a bag of sugar, which he knew Long Knife loved, and three cups, then joined his foster father and walked down to the edge of the meadow and the trees beyond.

Dan saw Long Knife stand as they approached and saw him urge a woman to her feet. She held an infant in her arms. "Greetings, Uncle, and young Dan—although not so small now."

Dan grinned and waved. "Howdy, Knife. Long time no see… where you been so long?"

Knife looked down and away—a uniquely Indian

gesture meaning Bad Medicine, terrible news; and Jake gently took ahold of Dan's shoulder, shaking his head as if demanding the boy be silent. Dan took the hint and stared at his old friend in dismay.

Looking up, Long Knife said, "I have many stories to tell, but first I want you to meet my wife, Golden Fawn, and my son, Dark Moon." Knife's new wife was quite young, plump and round-faced but she had sweet eyes and clearly adored both her husband and her new baby.

She beamed with pride and handed her son to Knife's uncle. Jake took the baby and stared past its soft hide blanket into a face that made his heart ache with loss. This baby would have been kin to his own son, Little Elk, and the family resemblance was astonishing. "He's perfect, Fawn... Long Knife. May he grow to be a proud and mighty warrior."

Kneeling on one knee, Jake showed Dan Long Knife's son and the boy stared at the baby with wonder and delight. Dan had never held a baby and didn't want to start now (he was too sacred of dropping it), but he looked up at Knife and said, "You're a daddy now, Knife! Congratulations!"

Knife plucked the baby from Jake's hands and held him up to the pale morning sky. "May he be free! That is all I ask now." Handing the infant to its mother, he spoke with her a moment and she scurried to the closest tipi.

Turning back toward them, Long Knife said, "Jake, our tribe is no more. We are destroyed and fleeing U.S.

soldiers. Old Iron Horse is dead now, and my father, Black Bird, was killed at the Bighorn. I would have stayed until the end, but my father sent me to protect what was left of our tribe, after the U.S. Army pursued the consolidated Indian tribes. Most of our warriors perished in that war and those who did not die outright have fallen from illness and persecution since the Greasy Grass war."

Jake and Dan stared at the young Indian man, stricken with grief. A whole tribe of Cheyenne reduced to a mere handful of old men, women and small babies. Jake cleared his throat and asked, "What can we do to help?"

Long Knife gazed at the ground in front of his moccasins for a moment. "I know we bring you great danger, but I hoped you would give us shelter—at least for a little while. Give my people a chance to recover and grow strong again. Is that possible, old friend?"

Jake, knowing that harboring a renegade band of outlawed Injuns might cause him and Dan a great deal of trouble, and a whole bunch of undue attention, said, "Yes, of course, nephew. Dan and I will do whatever it takes to see your people whole again."

LONG KNIFE and what was left of his people did not stay for long. In fact, they left in the nick of time. Two and a half weeks after their arrival, a small battalion of U.S. cavalry arrived in the valley.

As Jake walked up to meet with the officer in charge, he did a quick mental evaluation of Long Knife's campsite and knew, instinctually, it was clean. No one could move as quickly, quietly or stealthily as the American Indian when necessary, and his friend had taken great pains to cover his people's tracks when they left.

Still, it was a close thing. They had only moved on two days earlier, and an enterprising scout could ride to the top of the mountain and maybe even see the small band of Indians making their way through the pass on their way south.

But this group of soldiers seemed like a tired bunch, and almost as dispirited as the Indians they pursued. The lieutenant in charge removed his cap as Jake approached and said, "Hello! Sorry if we're trespassing, but we're lookin' for a band of hostiles that were last seen heading your way. You haven't seen 'em, have you?"

Jake scratched his head. "Wahl, we see Injuns here and there but I'm not sure which ones you're referring to—be they Sioux, or Arapaho?"

The officer sighed. "Nah, these be Cheyenne... about twenty of them travelling south. Mostly old folks, squaws and children."

Jake grinned. "Sounds like a pretty fierce bunch, alright... my son and I better look sharp!" Belligerence towards Army troops was a sure-fire way to bring trouble down on your head, but Jake couldn't resist the barb.

The young lieutenant seemed to agree, however, and shook his head in disgust. "Yeah, seems like a waste of time to me as well. Still, we have our orders, and I'm honor bound to bring those war criminals to justice."

Jake was tempted to ask what the Indian's crime was, but thought he'd pressed his luck far enough. Nodding agreeably, he said, "Wahl, honestly, since that dust-up at the Little Bighorn we don't see many Injuns around anymore... which is just fine by me."

The Army officer turned around and waved his right hand in the air. Jake figured it was a—'let's round it up and get moving gesture, and sure enough the six soldiers behind the lieutenant mounted their horses.

Turning back to face Jake, the young soldier said, "Looks like you got yourself a nice spread here..." He studied the farm, the small barn, the livestock and young Dan, who was weeding the corn patch about 100-feet away. A frown crossed his face and he continued.

"Keep in mind, sir, the Army is now authorized to seize land from settlers who give shelter to renegade Indians. I'd hate to see this purty little ranch land in the hands of 'Uncle Sam' just cuz someone felt sorry for a band of scrawny Injuns..."

Jake's heart started pounding loudly in his chest and it took every ounce of acting skill he'd ever possessed to maintain a bland, unconcerned expression as he faced the young officer down. Nodding, he drawled, "I'd hate to see that happen, too. Good thing my boy and I are well off the beaten path and we haven't seen neither hide nor tail of any natives lately." He clapped his hat on his head, adding, "But rest assured, if'n we do, I'll be sure to send word…"

He peered into the lieutenant's eyes, "How *would* I get word to you?"

The officer grinned. "As luck would have it, a new garrison has been built just outside of Laramie. If you catch wind of Indian movement around these parts, you just skedaddle into town and let one of the officers in charge know, okay?"

Like hell I will, Jake thought, but said, "You can bet on it, sir."

Then the Army boys wheeled their horses and rode back they way they came as Jake watched, eyes narrowed in anger.

Chapter Twenty-Four

1882

ARCHIE BANYON STAYED on for about two and a half years, but to Dan it seemed like only days. Although he'd resisted his instructions at first, thinking his teacher's silly old books and papers a big waste of time, he found out that learning things was... fun!

With Mr. Banyon's gentle persuasion, Dan learned about British kings and queens, French emperors, Roman conquerors and Greek philosophers. He learned the ins and outs of all the major wars fought throughout history (most of which smacked of money grubbing- that or religion, which also somehow smacked of money-grubbing.)

He studied the war campaigns of great military leaders such as Genghis Khan, and Hannibal, Caesar and Napoleon Bonaparte. He learned that hubris was the Achilles' heel of most battle commanders and that power was only as vibrant as the loyalty of a war leader's troops.

He studied American politics (and swore he'd avoid politicians on general principles if humanly possible), and learned about the earth itself; it's soil, and rocks, trees, flowers, and the many vast oceans that covered the planet's surface. He learned about the many fishes in those briny seas and about the vast array of animals on the planet's land masses. He even learned a little about the heavens above- the stars, the moon, and the other planets that rotated around the big, yellow sun.

The information he received from his little teacher seemed almost too outrageous to be true, sometimes, but Archie assured him that the world was a strange and wonderous thing, which few understood to the fullest.

Jake studied advanced math, which he hated at first and then grew to love and he read the classics late into the night until Jake yelled at him to stop wasting candle wax and GET SOME SLEEP!

He worked hard on his chores every morning and worked with Archie every evening after supper. But from about three in the afternoon until supper he worked with Jake's guns. He thought he already knew what he needed to know to get along in a gun fight, but Jake wanted more than that from him. He wanted nothing less than a master-shootist.

Whenever the guns came out, Archie would stuff his ears with plugs of beeswax and flee down to the creek. But, once the guns were put away for the night, he would come up to the house with his latest lesson already mapped out, and a wide, excited smile on his face.

His joy in teaching was infectious, and Dan would sit down at the table in anticipation of what strange new thing he might learn next. Jake sat inside as well, learning new things along with his foster son, glad to know that before he went under, he finally had a chance to learn more about this big old world he'd often found so inhospitable and threatening.

Then, one day in October, Archie announced he was leaving. He had a new student, he said, and needed to go now and attend to her needs. Dan was devastated, but Jake knew the old man had stayed far past the time he'd been paid for.

"But... but can't you stay?" Dan asked. He'd grown fond of the quirky old man, and could hardly imagine being without his cheery presence, but Archie shook his head. "No, Dan. It's time I go now... I have other pupils who need my instructions, okay?"

Dan nodded miserably, until he felt the pointy tip of Jake's elbow dig into his ribs. "Mind yer manners, son, and say thank you to Mr. Banyon for all his good teachings."

Realizing he was acting like a spoiled child, Dan recovered his wits and said, "Yes!, Thank you so much, Mr. Banyon. I never knew that learning could be so much fun. I appreciate it."

Archie grinned. "It was my great pleasure, Dan. You

are very smart, and a fine student. Now, I have left two of my favorite books behind for you to study... they are the study of life and how the decisions we make can sometimes affect the world around us. Read them and learn."

With those words, he was gone, and Dan stared after him with sorrow. Then he walked into the house where Jake was gazing down at two beautiful leather books. One was called *Moby Dick* and the other, *The Count of Monte Cristo*.

Dan would read those books over and over, until the pages grew brittle and torn, and their spines creaked with the strain.

———

IT WAS A LONG HARD WINTER, made more so by the sudden, fierce onslaught of Jake's illness. What had once been a general ache and malaise was now a howling inferno of pain, nausea and a loss of control over his body. Jake muscled through the cold of November, the blowing snows of December, and the deep, bone-chilling freeze of January. But by February 1883, he was bedridden, and Dan was the only thing that kept him from death's door.

Dan was bewildered. He had known that his foster-father was slowing down and sleeping a lot more than usual, but he'd figured it was just old age, or a bad chest cold and "time" would heal Jake up and make him feel better and stronger.

He was wrong, though, and kept asking Jake what he could do to help. Jake just shrugged and said there was nothing to be done about it, but keep his medicine coming. Finally, the medicine ran out, and Dan told Jake he needed to go into town to fetch more from the doctor.

Jake, awake and fairly lucid, said, "No, you can't ride out in this snow. Just let it be, son."

Dan felt a chill run through his body. Jake was a mere shadow of his original self—as thin as a rail, pale, ashen skin and eyes sunk so far into his face they resembled black raisins in white pudding. "No, sir. I know the trail is open about two miles from here... I could use old Jonesy to bust a trail. He would like it!"

Jake shook his head, grimacing. "Nah, 'twold be a waste of time and money. Just bring me a bottle of that hooch I got stashed and bring a chair on over by the bed. I got some things I want to talk to you about."

Dan' s hands shook as he brought a wooden chair over by Jake's bed. He set a bottle of whiskey and a glass on a side table and poured his adopted Pa a glass of the spirits. He realized now that a hideous, gray shadow hovered over Jake's brow like a scepter and was about to carry his foster-father away.

Tears filled his eyes and he wiped them away before Jake could see. He'd finally come to terms with the loss of his own family and had even been happy with his present circumstances, but now Jake was leaving him as well, and Dan didn't know how he could carry on by himself.

Jake took a slug of his whiskey and laid back on his pillow with a ragged sigh. "Don't cry for me, Dan. This has been a long time coming and I'm ready to go under…"

Dan was suddenly incensed. "Well, I ain't! What's wrong with you, anyway? I thought you just had a cold or something, and now you say you're dying… why?"

Jake shook his head. "Wahl, it ain't no cold, that's for sure. Doc says I have a cancer—deep inside. There's nothing he can do for me, except try to keep me comfortable—which he has done to the best of his ability."

Dan was still mad. "How long have you known about this? Maybe, if you'd told me sooner, something could have been done!"

Jake was already shaking his head, and he wore a small smile. "No, son. You don't cure something like this, okay? It just can't be done." His eyes closed for a moment and then he fixed his gaze on Dan.

"Now, quit pestering me about it and listen to what I have to say. It's important. I found out about this during the market fair when we were in Laramie, after I was examined by the town doctor. Soon as I found out that there weren't no cure, I headed down to the bank and got these…" His hand, as thin and scrawny as a skeleton's gestured toward a satchel that sat by the end of his bed.

"Bring that up here, so I can reach it," he demanded.

Dan pulled the heavy carpetbag up off the floor and placed it on the bed. Jake reached inside and pulled out a loose-leaf, leather notebook. He handed it to the boy and said, "Take a look at these papers."

Dan pulled a sheath of heavy documents out and studied them as Jake continued. "This is the deed to the ranch and a list of my earthly belongings. It's all yours, son. There's about $2000 in cash at this same bank and it's in your name. That oughta see you through if your careful and don't start drinking or gamblin'. I can tell you, for a certainty, that nuthin' eats into a man's wallet like too much booze or the call of the cards."

Dan's tears were flowing freely now, and he kept shaking his head in denial. Why, just last week he and Jake were busting a gut laughing as one of their sows chased an unruly barn cat that had stolen a chicken bone right out of the pig's mouth. That *was* just last week, wasn't it? Or, was that a few weeks ago?

Jake reached out and touched Dan's sleeve. "You're gonna be okay, ya know. I'm sorry about it, and for leaving you alone, but you're all set." He took another deep pull off his glass, adding, "Hit me again, won't you?"

SOON AFTER, Jake fell into a deep sleep, or what would later be called a coma. Dan had no idea what to do. He was sorely tempted to deny Jake's orders and ride hell bent for leather into Laramie for more medicine, but he was afraid that the moment he left Jake would wake up and need his assistance.

So, he paced back and forth; put cool compresses on Jake's brow, added more blankets to his bed when the man commenced to shivering, and tried to keep from bawling like a new-born calf. Jake stayed under for almost three days, and then he awoke, and stared at Dan with luminous green eyes that glittered with fever in the fitful firelight.

"Dan... come here," he whispered.

Dan almost jumped out of his skin when he heard Jake's voice... he was sure that the man was ready to breathe his last. In fact, twice over the last couple of hours, Jake had stopped breathing altogether. Only a few soft slaps and fervent hugs had revived the man enough to take a deep gasp of air.

Dan ran to Jake's side, and pleaded, "Jake, tell me, PLEASE! What can I do to help?"

Jake smiled and cupped his big hand around Dan's right cheek. "Lookit you... handsome as a devil, even counting your scars. You'll be able to find yourself a good woman, and a pretty one too."

Dan shook his head. "I don't want a woman, Pa. I just want you to get well!"

Jake's eyelids fell shut and then he startled himself awake again. Gazing at Dan he said, "My time is short, kid. So, listen up, okay?"

Dan nodded, and wiped running snot from his nose. Jake didn't care for tears and had said, more than once, "all that energy bawlin' your eyes out? That energy can be used for better things—like stayin' alive."

Jake studied his face again and continued. "I think I already told you this farm is yours now?"

Dan agreed, and the older man said, "Good. Now, I think you're a bit young yet to run a farm like this, but you'll do what you see fit. Just want you to know that there's a young couple living down by the Johnsons who are looking for a little place like this. Their name is Kidwell... Rhett and Bonnie Kidwell, out of Missouri. They seem to be good folks. If you were to sell out, I think they would be good custodians of the land. Also, they are willing to lease; which would mean they pay you a small monthly rate to run the place, and keep any profits they make, but have first right to buy should you want to sell out."

He started coughing, hard, and his eyes bugged as he pounded his chest with a frail fist. Dan scooted around behind him and helped Jake to sit up against the headboard, so he could take air in easier. His pale face turned gray even as Dan watched with dread.

A few minutes passed as Jake collected his scattered wits, and then he reached out and took Dan's hand in his. "There's one last thing I gotta get off my chest before I go... you ain't going to like it, but you need to know." His eyelids drooped, showing purple bruises, but then Jake's green gaze was on him again.

"I was one of them, Dan. One of the gang that killed your ma and pa and brother and all the rest of those pilgrims. I'm sor..."

Dan pulled his hand away from Jake's grasp with a

gasp. "What? What do you mean, you were one of them?"

Jake nodded slowly, "Wahl, right at that particular moment, I was no longer a member of Heck's gang... I was making my escape when you practically ran over me—remember?"

Dan nodded, but his heart had turned cold and he stared at Jake with a mixture of love and loathing.

Jake studied the boy's face and sighed. "I had no part in killing your family, kid, but that ain't no excuse for the things I done with Heck Giddings's outlaw gang. I done plenty to earn me a one-way ticket to hell."

Dan had once acknowledged to himself that Jake might have been an outlaw at one time, but now, as it pertained to him and his long-dead family, the hurt was too immediate. He stood up from the bed and stared down at his foster-father. "Why? Why would you do such terrible things, Jake? I trusted you and now, I... I..."

Jake smiled in sadness. "Honestly, it all seems like some one else's memories. I just know that after my wife and child died, I was so angry. It seemed like life had dealt me nuthin' but bad hands, and I wanted to strike back, somehow. Take what I wanted, when I wanted it, even if that meant going about it all wrong."

Dan paced back and forth, wringing his hands. "Well, I wish you never told me what you did! I can't... I just don't know why you had to tell me you were the worst kind of outlaw!"

Jake nodded. "I told you because I love you and you deserved to know the truth. Also, I needed you to know that Hector never forgets a slight. I slighted him, Dan, when I took off. I disrespected him in front of his men, and he does not forgive."

Jake started coughing again, but this time his lungs were about played out, and the man simply lay on his bed and wheezed. After a few minutes passed and Jake had gathered enough energy to talk again, he said, "I never once told Heck about this place, so we've managed to stay safe, so far. But I heard that the Giddings's gang is back in the area. It's bigger and stronger than ever, apparently, and I heard that Heck has been asking around about me."

He studied the eighteen-year-old face in front of him and marveled at the halo that seemed to surround the boy's head. He knew it was just lantern light putting a golden glow around him, but he honestly felt that Dan was some kind of angel sent to guide him on his way.

He sought out the boy's eyes and said, "Anybody who has to come to know us over the last few years knows that you are my son. Please, don't let Heck Giddings get his hands on you. I hope that you will move on from here—at least for a while, until Hector and his men move on. Can you do that for me, son?"

Dan didn't want to agree with Jake on anything right now… he was too shocked and too angry with the man he'd grown to love to forgive such a betrayal of his trust. He stood staring at the wall above the cook stove and silently counted to twenty—thinking to make Jake wait for the answer he clearly wanted.

Then he turned around to say okay, he'd make himself scarce, but saw that the man he loved with all his heart was lying dead on his bed with a small smile and his wide green eyes fixed on some distant eternity.

Chapter Twenty-Five

DAN SPENT ANOTHER FOUR MONTHS ON THE SMALL ranch before moving on. After Jake died, he wasn't sure what to do, but he knew he couldn't do any burying because the ground was frozen solid. He did, however, wrap his pa in several old blankets and put him up in the barn loft for safekeeping, at least until the ground thawed and he could give Jake a proper burial.

He wasn't sure, until he tried, if he could even lift the man who had always, in his mind, seemed bigger than life, but Jake had lost so much weight, he felt no heavier than a child. Salty tears ran in a steady flow down Dan's cheeks as he placed his pa's body close to the barn's outside wall, so Jake would freeze and stay as frozen as possible until spring.

Then, he went about his business and tried not to dwell on how lonesome he was. He continued to tend to the trap lines—his and Jake's both—and marveled at how thick and glossy the animal's pelts were. It had been a long and icy winter, but God had seen fit to clothe his beasts in thick, furry splendor so they wouldn't freeze in the winter's cold.

At any rate, Dan knew his pelts would fetch a high-price at the next fair and would supplement his inheritance handsomely. He wasn't sure, yet, what he was going to do, but he thought that first; he would go and see the Kidwells and find out if they were still interested in leasing his pa's place. He figured he would go ahead and sell a few heads of beef, and most of the sheep to the Kidwells or anyone else who would pay a fair price.

They had four horses, three donkeys, one ornery old mule and an assortment of ducks and chickens. He would take two of the horses—Old Jonesy for packing and Jake's fine roan gelding. Then, he would sell the rest and go—North into Montana or even Idaho, where the gypsies had gone.

He wanted to honor his foster-father's wishes and make himself scarce. Also, if Jake was correct about his old boss, Heck Giddings, he did not want to die at the hands of an outlaw gang! Still, Dan knew he needed to hone his skills and get better at pistol-work, and that would take time and practice.

He spent most evenings tending to his plews and using his newly minted mathematics to figure out how much he was worth. Many days, he worked on a small plot of land on a rise behind the house. It was up on a small hill and benefited from the most sunlight year-round, so the ground began to thaw even as the rest of the valley snoozed under four inches of old ice and dirty snow.

The ground was still firm, though, and digging a six-foot hole was slow going. But Dan plugged away, day by day and finally, around the 10th of April and after six days of warm weather, he finished the burial plot, and just in time, too. The warm sun had started to thaw Jake's body, and a keen, terrible odor was wafting down from the barn's loft.

Dan climbed slowly up the ladder and tried not to quake with fear. For some reason, his imagination was running away with his thoughts, and he felt like Jake's spirit was hovering over his every move. He kept telling himself to stop acting like a scare-baby but grasping Jake's body in his arms and feeling his pa's remains shift liquidly, he almost dropped his load and ran outside, screaming in fright.

Gritting his teeth against his rising panic, Dan hauled Jake's body down the steps and put it into the back of the buckboard. Then he drove up the hill to the grave he'd dug. He carefully placed Jake's body in the gravesite and scrambled out of the hole. Then he stood still and murmured, "Thank you, sir. I know you did some bad things, but you did right by me, and I'll never forget you. I loved you as my pa, and I'll go to my grave knowing how hard you tried to redempt yourself."

The boy stood staring out over his small homestead and made a promise. Looking back down at Jake's blanket-wrapped body, he added, "I know you think you're headed for hell, Jake, but I don't. It might have taken a while, but you paid for your sins... I know you did. But, one thing seems clear. That old boss of yours, Hector Giddings? He still walking around breathing, and that don't seem right, nor fair."

Dan trembled as he realized the enormity of his intentions. He'd been thinking about little else since Jake had disclosed the truth on his deathbed. Still, his mind was made up and he told Jake now; "I ain't... I mean, I'm not ready yet, sir. I know that. I need more practice and more experience to do what's right. But, I'm going after Heck Giddings and his gang of killer outlaws. It's not right that he chased you all the way to the grave and seems intent on getting his stupid, prideful revenge."

The boy's bright blue eyes blazed as he grasped ahold of the shovel that stood, close by on a mound of dirt. "Well, sir, he's going to get his revenge alright, but the revenge will be coming from me—not him! It might take a while—a few years even, but the last thing that man is going to see is Jacob Conrad's son staring down the wrong end of a pistol at him. Right before he goes under—forever!"

Chapter Twenty-Six

TWO MONTHS LATER, DAN HEADED INTO LARAMIE WITH a wagon-load of trade goods. He had over a hundred furs, eggs, leather goods and assorted dishware and pots and pans to sell at the upcoming fair. Jonesy was pulling the wagon and Jake's horse, Honey, was tied on back. In two days, Dan would meet up with Rhett Kidwell, who had decided to lease his farm, and turn the wagon over to him and his wife.

He felt both frightened and exhilarated. Being alone on familiar ground was one thing... heading out into the unknown was quite another. Still, he had a plan, and enough cash money to implement it. He just hoped his goods would fetch a fair price and he wouldn't run into trouble at the bank when he withdrew a thousand dollars from his account.

He twitched the reins over Jonesy's rump. The lazy old horse was, as usual, taking advantage of Dan's inattention and heading for a clump of ripe weeds by the side of the trail into town. "You get on, Jonesy! Lazy old dog..." Dan hollered and grinned as the horse turned his big head and snorted at him with disdain before picking up his pace.

He saw the town ahead, and spied a few smokes rising into the air behind it. He'd heard rumors that the fair might be cancelled this year, due to an over-abundance of pelts, but Dan hadn't believed it. There were too many other supplies needed in this part of the country besides furs to cancel such a big market. Relieved that his suspicions were correct, he drove slowly down Main Street and saw that the general shape of the big meet was changed; smaller yes, but more densely packed.

As he drove his wagon close to the crowd to park, his nose wrinkled at the smell of spirits, cow manure, sweat, and unwashed bodies. Even as he sneezed in disgust, other more attractive fragrances over-rode the noisome odors like; popcorn, cotton candy, the sharp smell of Sarsaparilla, and sweet cakes.

Dammit!, Dan thought, and jerked the reins back as he saw that Jonesy was helping himself to someone else's hay bale.

"Hey, you better curb yer horse before I charge him with theft!" A large black man stood behind several bales of hay, and although his words were spoken with authority, his eyes were filled with mirth, and Dan realized he was just kidding.

Dan hauled back on the reins, and Jonesy was

forced to retreat from the tempting treat. "Sorry, sir. This horse is a menace to hay piles everywhere!"

The man smiled, and his teeth gleamed brightly against his dark skin. "Just like every good hoss, I think. A well-treated horse ain't ashamed to show his appetite."

Liking the man, a lot, Dan grinned back and said, "Well, that's Jonesy's main problem… he's spoiled rotten and shows off his appetite too much!"

"My name be Jonathon Leggy. I'm a blacksmith. I haven't fired my forge up yet, but if you need any shoeing done, I'm your man."

Dan said, "Pleased to make your acquaintance. My name is Daniel Monroe."

"Nice to meet you, Dan You be selling all that stuff in your wagon?" Leggy asked.

Dan said, "Yes sir—hopefully all of it. Where's the best place to park my rig, do you know?"

Leggy nodded and glanced behind him and to the right. "If'n I was you I'd park over there…" He pointed his finger at an empty piece of real estate toward the back. "I heard that the gypsies are heading in today and once they do, you'll be right in the middle of the action. Plus, there ain't no innocent piles of hay lying around over there!"

Dan grinned and said, "Thank you, sir. I'm heading over there now."

The big man grinned and waved. "Hope you get a good price for your goods. Take care, now."

Dan drove around the milling crowd and parked a

distance away—feeling a little foolish. Folks would have to walk clear over to where he and his trade goods sat alone, and he wondered momentarily whether Leggy knew what he was talking about, or if he'd been had.

Still, he set his goods out on the ground in front of his wagon and sat down to eat an apple and a bacon sandwich he'd made and put away in his personal stores. No one came, though, and he was really beginning to think he should move back toward the crowd, but then he heard a clatter behind him and looked up to see about a dozen bright gypsy wagons heaving into the pasture behind him.

Leggy was right! Dan thought with glee as several people started walking his way, or more specifically, toward the gypsy's wagons.

Dan looked closely to see if Manny and his father were in the gypsy's train but couldn't tell. Plus, some folks had stopped and were now staring at his trade goods with interest.

"These are good-lookin' plews, son. Where's your pa… and how much does he want for them?"

Dan had worried about this. Even though he stood almost 5'11 and weighed in at a respectable 185 pounds, he still sported a baby-face with fresh white skin and eyes as round and blue as any girl's. Even his beard was scarce, and he'd shaved off his efforts to look older the day before.

Dan had a vague memory of his own Pa's glorious

whiskers, and had assumed he'd be just as blessed but, so far, except for a few stragglers, his face was as smooth as a baby's bottom.

He answered the man's query with as much dignity as possible. "My pa isn't here today, sir. He put these trade goods in my hands to sell. So, how does one beaver token or $2 a piece sound? That would be for beaver, otter and mink. The other, bigger hides—I have three deer hides, one moose and one elk hide—would go for a buck each and a buck and two bits for the moose and elk. I have a scale right here."

Dan felt himself being scrutinized but eventually, the folks started buying his hides and plews for the asking price. A few tried to bicker him down, but Dan just shrugged and said, "My Pa set the price, gentlemen. It ain't up to me to change his orders…"

He felt kinda bad about using his "fictional" Pa to keep his customers in line, but he knew that 'human nature' would—more often than not—compel the buyer to cheat as much as possible to get the best price. Dan also knew that a "wet-behind the ears" boy would be viewed as "Cheap Bait" to most buyers.

All in all, Dan did well on his first day. He sold most of his hides, all his eggs, and had cut his cookware by half. It was starting to get dark when he put his remaining wares back in the wagon, pulled a heavy tarp over them and sat down in front of his small cook fire for dinner.

Just as he jumped into the wagon to get some shut-eye, he heard the soft sound of guitar music rising into the dusky air. *Tomorrow,* he thought, *tomorrow, I'll go and see if Manny is there...*

Chapter Twenty-Seven

HE WOKE UP EARLY THE NEXT MORNING. LOOKING around, he saw that most of the folks in the encampment were still sleeping, except for a few early birds, who were building up their cook fires and walking toward a large tarp which hid a few out houses.

Looking farther to his right, Dan gazed over at the gypsy wagons and saw cook fires sparking in the cool morning air. Two small, swarthy men were moving amongst the horses with full barrows of feed.

He threw wood on his own fire and started a pot of coffee. Then, he fed Honey and Jonesy oats and hay, and filled their small, metal trough with fresh water. By the time he finished and sat back down, the fire was sending out warmth and his coffee was perking.

He'd arrived late to the fair, and many of the wagons he'd noticed yesterday had already taken off. Even as he watched, Dan saw more folks loading up their remaining wares and getting ready to go home.

He sighed with relief... thanks to Mr. Leggy, most of his goods had already sold. He had a few more items to trade, but this time he wanted to trade for gunpowder, bullet casings and maybe, a spyglass.

All things he thought would come in handy for wherever he decided to go. And knowing that the Kidwells would arrive the next morning for the wagon made Dan resolve to trade his goods for the valuables he needed as quickly as possible.

He put a couple pieces of dried backstrap into his cast-iron skillet with a little water and let the meat warm as he contemplated the best way to trade his remaining goods. He didn't really want to drive his wagon all over Sunday, but also didn't think he could carry his remaining hides to the vendors. *Hmmm,* he wondered.

He picked his pan up off the coals with a piece of old, scorched hide and had just tucked into his break-fast when he heard footsteps approaching. Looking up, he grinned with delight. "Manny! I hoped you were here. I was just fixing to head over there and say hi!"

Manny Amaya smiled in return. "¡Hola, Daniel! I almost didn't know it was you. I was looking for you and your father..." The young man's expression showed his concern. His old granny had told him that she'd seen the shadow of death sitting on Jake's shoul-ders and had predicted that Dan's father was not long for this world.

Even as he asked, he saw swift tears fill Dan's eyes,

but they were quickly wiped away. "Yes, my pa passed on a few months ago. I'm alone now."

His words were nothing more than the truth, but uttering them sounded so pathetic, he added, "That's okay though... I'm alright."

Manny didn't agree, but he let it pass. Instead, he said, "I am very sorry for your loss, Daniel. Hey, the women are cooking a big meal. Why don't you come with me? My sister made bread last night and promised me a whole loaf!"

Dan smiled and said, "Sure—uh, thanks!" He stood up, wondering if it was safe to leave the wagon and his remaining trade goods alone.

Manny said, "Just hop up there and we'll drive your rig over to my camp."

Dan spilled what was left of his water and coffee over the hot coals of his fire while Manny backed Jonesy up to the wagon's traces. He spoke soft words in the old horse's ears as he eased the harness over its head and Jonesy complied without even a snort of protest. Dan vowed to learn some of the gypsy's tricks when dealing with horseflesh.

As they drove the thousand or so feet to the gypsy encampment, Dan saw men setting up starting and ending lines for their horse races, and he noticed tables being set-up for the day's customers. He knew that many men and women in the crowd were anxiously waiting for the gypsy's potions and elixirs and even the fortunes told by the wise women in the train.

Gratified by his acceptance into the "Traveler's"

clan, he drove his wagon around the main campground and toward the tree line and small creek behind that. As they made their way, Manny asked, "Daniel, do you really know how to shoot those guns of yours?"

Dan felt almost offended, but one look at the smaller boy's face revealed that Manuel meant no offence but was simply curious.

"Yeah, I do," he answered. "Jake made me learn. I practice every day, even now that he's gone... I didn't want to let him down, you see."

Manny nodded, with a grin. "Well, reason I ask is, my Papá wondered if you were any good. See, we were thinking of adding a couple more acts to our show. Some of us had the chance to see Buffalo Bill Cody's Wild West show in the Dakotas. Have you seen it?"

Dan shrugged and shook his head.

"Well, mi amigo," Manny exclaimed. "It was *muy bueno*! Many horses and tame Indians and many great shooters... even *señoritas*! That's when my Papá said we should try to find us a good shootist. We remembered you, with your two pistols and thought, 'A boy with his guns!' Yes! We would pack 'em in, just like Buffalo Bill! Do you agree?"

Dan didn't know if he agreed or not, but he smiled and said, "Well, can I think about it for a little bit? Don't know if I'm good enough."

Manny nodded, "Si. Mi Papá, and the Rom's leaders would need to watch you shoot before they hired you, see? Maybe later today, after the crowd goes home, you can shoot some targets and show my Papá what you can do? I would love to bring you with us when we leave… keep you close as a friend!"

Looking Dan up and down, he added, "Besides, right now, there are more women than men in our group. One reason we are so late in arriving is we lost two axles and three wheels coming here. You are a big boy, and know your way around wagons and horses, see? Your strong back would be of great use to us!" Manny looked as pleased as punch; like he'd just solved all his people's problems with one try.

Dan grinned and wondered if this wasn't just what the Doctor ordered or, in his case, Jake. There would be safety in numbers, and maybe some protection if he followed the gypsies from one place to the next. Maybe he could slip away, unnoticed, before his pa's nemesis, Heck Giddings, even knew he existed!

Chapter Twenty-Eight

DAN SPENT MOST OF THE MORNING SELLING THE REST OF his wares (mainly to the gypsies) and at about 1:00 he decided to walk the half mile into town to visit the bank. He wanted to turn his beaver chips into cash and pull about half his inheritance out, so he could line his pockets with enough money to properly flee the area.

In addition, he wanted to buy a money-belt and a telescope. He had looked, in vain, for the leather artist, Jerome Smalley, but he was nowhere to be found. He wondered what had happened to the old man and couldn't help but grieve. He had only met the man once, but he was as old as the hills even then... Dan wouldn't be surprised if Jerome had gone under.

Many wagons passed him by as he walked slowly into town. Most folks were smiling with pleasure, but some seemed downcast—as if they'd not made out well at the big meet. Looking ahead, Dan saw the brick bank. He had taken some care with his appearance and hoped now that his signature would stand as a surety to allow access to his funds.

He stepped up onto the boardwalk and walked through the front door of the bank. He was taken by surprise by how big the crowd was—there were three long lines of people and there was a busy teller at all three windows. He stepped into the shortest queue and thought, *Well, it ain't no wonder the bank is busy... all these people want to either take their money out or put it in after the fair—just like me.*

The bank manager, Earl McNally; watched the proceedings with pleasure. He walked back and forth behind the tellers and took note of the fortunes being placed into the bank's big safe. Every transaction, whether it was cash coming in, or cash walking out needed his signature, and he took his time going over every document as if all that money was his... which, in a way, it was.

McNally was as crooked as a stick and had made a fortune in his dirty, high interest dealings with the people in and around Laramie for the last ten years. He was also a silent partner in more than half the stagecoach and train robberies in this part of southern Wyoming. He mainly helped Heck Billings' band of crooks by letting them know when coaches and trains were either bringing bank notes into or out of the Laramie branch of the bank. His usual cut was 10 percent of the money stolen. In addition, most of his help had been hired for their willingness to cooperate in his nefarious schemes for a paltry one percent of the take.

All but one man. His name was Monty Smyth. Monty was the grown son of the bank's original owner, Arthur Smyth, who had taken great pride in his bank and how well it protected the vulnerable citizens in the area. Old Arthur had decided to sell his concerns when he was seventy-years-old, but the one condition he'd demanded of the buyers was that they keep his son on as a teller.

Monty was a simple man and had always been a bit slow in the brainpan, but he was a good man and as honest as the day was long. He was the one man who did not over-charge customers regarding the bank's liquid and predatory interest rates. The customers appreciated his honesty and many of them would only do business with him. That was why his line that day was the longest of all and Dan was standing in a shorter and much quicker queue.

It took a while, but he finally made his way to the high, marble counter and placed his leather bag in front of a teller named Marvin Little. Little was almost as big a crook as his boss but not nearly as cheerful. He'd been involved in McNally's racket for four years now and thought he should be making more money than he did. It did not occur to him that McNally thought Little was as much a dupe as the bank's customers.

It was turning into a long, difficult day and Little was hungry and irritable. When he glanced up at the owner of the small leather bag of coin, bills and beaver chips, he glared at the boy in front of him. *Well, here's a real Mountain Billy, if I ever saw one*, he thought resentfully as he studied the young man's hand-made leather clothing, his scratched-up face and smelt the odor of horse emanating off him.

"What d'ya want?" he snarled.

Dan's eyes got big and he couldn't help but wonder... *did I do something wrong?* Jake had always been the one to go to the bank, so he wasn't sure how to go about turning his coin and chips into bills, but he'd been watching the other customers and he was following their lead.

"Um... just want this turned into cash, please, sir. And I want to make a withdrawal from my existing account. Dan Monroe's the name."

Suddenly, a heavy ledger hit the wooden floor with a loud bang. A few of the customers gasped, thinking that a rifle shot was roaring through the crowd, but giggled in relief as they saw McNally bend over with a grimace to pick up the heavy notebook.

"Sorry folks, fingers clumsy as feathers today..." he said loudly, both to cover his blush *and* his excitement. Dan Monroe! Son of Jake Conrad—could it really be him? Heck had put a bounty on the kid's head—a cool $500 for information on him and his whereabouts. And here he was now! He placed the ledger on his desk and turned around to give Little a hand.

Marvin Little also knew who Dan Monroe was and his attitude changed instantly. He smiled and said,

"Well, now... how do you do? I would be happy to help with your bag of coin and chips but our bank manager, Mr. McNally, would need to take over to access your account, okay?"

It suddenly seemed as if every eye in the bank's lobby was staring him down and Dan, acutely embarrassed, nodded mutely. He stood still as the teller counted his coin, beaver chips and cash money into a respectable $79. He put his money back into the leather pouch and, looking past the teller's right shoulder, he saw that the bank manager was staring at him with cold eyes.

He gulped, nervously, thinking, *Maybe I'm doing it wrong?* All Jake had said in those horrid, final days was, "Your signature will work fine, Dan. Just make sure you go through Monty Smyth's line. He's honest, and he won't try to cheat ya..."

Dan's face turned red as he remembered, too late, what his pa had said. The man, Mr. Smyth by his name tag, was staring at him as well, and looked worried. "ER... hum..." Smyth squeaked. "I was witness to Mr. Conrad's inheritance to his son. Perhaps, I should take over from here?"

McNally spun on his heels and barked, "Smyth! What do you think you're doing? Can't you see we're busy?"

Poor, simple Monty blushed as the harsh words echoed around the lobby and the people in his queue hissed with displeasure. They had, indeed, been standing in line for quite a while now and deserved his prompt attention. Still, he *knew*, just *knew* in his gut that the poor boy was about to be robbed by the very devil, himself!

Monty had been happy and relieved to keep his position at the bank when his dear old dad had sold the bank. He knew he didn't have the smarts to run the place, but his father had set him up with a nice inheritance and made sure he could keep working at the job he'd grown to love.

It was too bad Arthur had died before Monty had a chance to tell him he'd sold out to a bunch of crooks! Gulping nervously, he mumbled, "Sorry sir... of course, I will help our customers... of course."

Turning to Dan, McNally let out an oily smile and said, "Please, come into my office. We'll get you *all* sorted out."

Dan smiled in relief as he walked through a gate and followed the banker into the back room. He thought, *Good, it looks like I'm going to get my money, after all.*

He didn't see the wicked grin McNally wore as he walked toward the bank's big vault and felt the rooms two iron doors slam behind him.

Chapter Twenty-Nine

AFTER A MOMENT OR TWO OF SHOCKED BEWILDERMENT, Dan ran to the two, metal doors and said, "Hey! What are you doing? Let me out!"

No answer from the other side of the door, and Dan started to panic. He remembered the strange, hostile glare in McNally's eyes, and the look of pity and concern in Mr. Smyth's gaze when the bank manager led him away into the back room. He knew, suddenly, that he was in BIG trouble, but didn't have a clue as to why.

After a couple seconds of paralysis, he stepped up to the heavy doors and started pounding his fists on the metal and screaming his head off. By the muffled acoustics, however, Dan knew that no one could hear his cries.

Frustrated, he looked over at several small, locked drawers by the far wall and saw that each showed a series of numbers and letters on the front. He pulled out his own number—8-68—CON and walked over to look at the corresponding numbers on one of the drawers... Yes! 8-68-Con beckoned to him and he tried to pull the drawer out of the wall, but it wouldn't budge. Then he saw the tiny key-hole and realized he needed a key to get into it, and it seemed more than likely, McNally held the only key that fit.

There was a stool in the far corner of the room, so he went and sat on it, waiting to see what was going to happen. And he sat... and sat some more, getting up occasionally to stretch his legs and holler out in frustration.

Once in a while, he heard footsteps approaching and could even, at odd moments, hear the crowd of people out in the lobby, but no one came to let him out. Finally, when he judged that four or five hours had passed, he got up again and started screaming at the top of his lungs.

This time, however, he heard footsteps and one of the two metal doors swung open a crack. McNally, holding a small silver pistol in his right hand, said, "Disarm yourself, Mr. Monroe, and slide your firearms across the floor to me."

"No!" Dan snapped. "What the heck is going on here? You've got me imprisoned and I don't know why!" Quick as a wink, without even giving it a second's thought, he pulled his own pistol and aimed it right between McNally's eyes.

You put *your* gun down and slide it to me!" Dan

hissed.

McNally's eyes grew wide and he swiftly pulled the door closed with a bang almost loud enough to cover the sound of Dan's bigger gun going off. Too late, Dan realized that the bullet wouldn't penetrate the metal, but simply flatten out—which it did. Then, the overhead light went out, and Dan sat in the darkness, wondering what was going on and why he was being held captive by the bank manager.

———

ABOUT TWO BLOCKS AWAY, in a run-down but stately old house, Monty Smyth sat in his father's favorite arm chair and fretted. He had been given the bum's rush as soon as the bank's doors closed this afternoon, even with all the sorting and accounting that needed doing after such a busy day, and he thought it had something to do with the boy's disappearance.

Granted, there was a back door to the bank that opened to the alleyway, but no one ever used it unless the stage pulled up to transfer money, and that wasn't supposed to happen for three more days.

And, customers weren't allowed! It was too close to the bank's vault and sensitive paperwork to let the public wander around back there with impunity. He should have seen Dan Monroe coming out from the back room, but although he'd kept his eyes peeled, there was no sign of him.

Monty feared that the boy had come to a bad end

because of his father's inheritance, and he didn't know what to do. The only thing that came to mind was using his father's old key to break into the bank himself.

It sometimes seemed like Arthur's demise and the banks purchase was perfectly coordinated. One thing following the other so rapidly that little things like the previous owner's old keys had been over-looked in the transfer. Monty would never consider using the old keys in his father's roll-top desk for criminal activities, but now... Making a sudden decision, Monty got up and put on his coat.

He was probably crazy, but Monty wanted to make sure that the boy was not still trapped at the bank. He had no doubt that McNally and his henchmen would, if humanly possible, get his hands-on Daniel Monroe's cash. There was little he could do about that, but if the kid's life was in danger, why... he thought, *I might be slow, but I'm not cruel. I need to make sure the kid's okay!*

Stepping outside, Monty gazed down the street to the bank. It was dark, and he saw no one loitering about, so he walked swiftly toward his place of work. He tried to spot a sheriff or deputy making his rounds, but the streets were quiet.

He took a deep breath and fitted the key into front door lock. Either the key was fouled with old dust and dirt, or McNally had finally gotten around to changing the locks, but the door wouldn't budge.

He broke into a sweat and tried again when a heavily accented voice growled, "Where is our friend... the boy named Daniel? What have you done with heem?"

Chapter Thirty

MONTY FELT HIS BLADDER LET GO AND WANTED TO SINK into the floor from shame. But fear overrode his embarrassment as the voice whispered, "Give me those keys, Meester. We shall see if you have hurt our freend."

Monty saw the glimmering flash of sharpened metal and saw the knife's blade, along with his old key enter the door's keyhole, and then he was hustled inside the bank by whoever had ahold of him. He squeaked, "It wasn't me who hurt that boy! I was coming to save him!"

A match was dragged across something and a candle lit up the faces of those who surrounded him. Gypsies! Four men and one teenager stood in the banks lobby and regarded him with dark sullen eyes. The smallest of the men wore a wide cloth belt and gold and silver decorated his neck and earlobes. "Where is he?" the little man hissed.

Monty stuttered. "I'm… not sure but I think he might be locked in the vault. You have the key—there in your hand. It's the big key…"

Pedro Amaya and Manuel studied the keys on the big ring and Pedro asked, "Which way?"

"That way, behind the counter and to the right," Monty answered.

Pedro scowled and said to his partners, "Bring him, or he might try to run…"

Monty was hustled along again as the group made their way through the cluttered, desk-filled area behind the counter and into the back room. As soon as they stepped through, Monty could hear a faint, familiar voice hollering behind the vaults big metal doors.

The little man in charge glanced at Monty and murmured, "Now we shall see if you are guilty, or not."

Monty worried about the fierce little man and his companions but mainly he was relieved. There was every possibility his boss had killed the kid for his cash, and he knew there would be no way to prove his innocence if that were the case.

One of the bigger men stepped forward and put the key in the lock. At the same moment, Manny yelled out, "Dan, it is us… me and my Papá and our friends are here to save you!"

It was a good thing he spoke up, because Dan was standing on the opposite side of the metal doors with both of his pistols in his hands. He had thought it might be that McNally guy and he wasn't going to go down without a fight.

He hollered with glee and gratitude. "Manny! Thanks for coming... the bank manager put me in here for some reason, and I was afraid he was gonna kill me!"

Dan stood there with a happy expression on his face. Manny ran up to him and said, "When you did not come back home, we feared the worst, so we came to rescue you! What happened?"

Dan shook his head. "I honestly don't know! I think that Mr. McNally didn't want to give me my money and he put me in here..." he shrugged in bewilderment.

"So, *this* man did not try to harm you?" Pedro asked.

Dan looked past his gypsy friends and saw Monty Smyth standing in the background being held firmly by both arms. "Mr. Smyth! What are you doing here? I'm sorry, my pa told me to deal only with you, but I forgot!"

Abruptly, the gypsies let him go, gave his keys back and went so far as to straighten his coat. "We are very sorry, Mr. Smyth," Pedro said, softly. "Seems you were trying to help our friend, not hurt him. I hope you are not injured?"

Monty shook his head. "No, I'm fine. But young Dan is correct about Mr. McNally. He is a crook of the first order and was surely trying to shake the boy down for his inheritance. Wouldn't be the first time, either!"

Pedro frowned. "Dan, did you get your money?"

Dan shook his head. "Nah, not my inheritance money. I did get almost $79 for my trade goods though! Here…" He handed the little leather bag to the older man. "For your troubles…"

Pedro stared at the bag and shook his head. "No. You keep this money—you earned it. Maybe, you can work for us, and help us and you pay us that way, eh?"

Dan's head was already nodding in the affirmative and his eyes gleamed with joy. "Yes, that would be good. Something is going on here and I don't think it's safe—not for me or even for you-if you're my friend.

Pedro said, "Well, we must be going before we are caught and tried as bank robbers, sí"

Dan said, "For sure."

Then Monty said, "Dan, I liked your father. He was always kind to me… So, I want you to have the money he left you. Here…" he put a key in the Conrad box and pulled out a large bundle of money. He studied a piece of notebook paper wrapped around the cash and said, "Yes. There is a little over $2000 here. That outta set you up for a while."

The gypsies watched, as Dan took the cash and tried to stuff it in his pockets. Then, he shrugged and handed half of it to Manny saying, "Help me with this, okay?"

Pedro turned to Monty and said, "You are a good man, Mr. Smyth. How are you going to explain this to your boss?"

Monty shrugged. "I don't know anything about it! He and his crew already think I'm as dumb as a post, why should they think anything different now?"

Pedro shrugged. The man was probably right.

Without further ado, the gypsies and Dan Monroe slipped out the back door and crept into the night. A little while later, after studying the deserted street, Monty Smyth did the same and slept like baby once he finally got home.

———

THE NEXT MORNING at about 6:30, which was a Friday, Heck Giddings stared into the vault room and then turned his cold, reptilian gaze on Earl McNally. McNally swallowed nervously, and stuttered, "I just don't know how he managed to escape, Sir! It's impossible!"

"Impossible? Hmmm," he glared. "I can't believe you made such a dumb decision. You shoulda just told me about him and let him go—we woulda got the money off him and then done away with him forever. Instead, you abducted him in the middle of a working day—with people here—and now he's in the wind with a story to tell!"

McNally stared at the floor. Giddings was right—it *was* a stupid move. For one thing, he hadn't noticed the kid was sporting two pistols—they were hidden under his long leather duster—and he'd almost pissed himself when those guns flew up into the air and pointed directly at his face.

Also, his abrupt decision had almost put a kink in the gangs' plans for today, and now a witness to his stupidity and greed was running around free! His knees shook with nerves. That $500 reward, though, had been too tempting and he'd made a snap decision that might very well cost him his job—or even his life!

"I'm... I'm sorry, Heck." Earl pleaded. "I knew you were coming in today, and I also knew how much you wanted to get your hands on that kid. I hustled him back here knowing no one could hear him yell, and that he'd be right handy when you showed up. I can't figure out how he managed to escape. It's a mystery to me!"

Heck studied the door locks and saw that they seemed in perfect working order. Turning around he asked, "How many keys belong to this bank, and who has access to them?"

"Why, there's only two sets, sir. I have the one set and the other set is under lock and key... in that last box on the wall."

"Let's have a look-see," Heck demanded.

Stepping up to the box, McNally put the corresponding key in the lock. Opening the lid with supreme confidence, Earl's mouth dropped open as he saw the empty space. There was supposed to be a thousand dollars in cash (the bank's daily operating funds), the deed of sale for the bank building, a city license to operate and an identical set of keys to the one he currently carried. But, the box was empty.

He had no way of knowing that Pedro, still worried about Mr. Smyth's complicity, had spirited the box's contents away. Mostly to keep Mr. Smyth safe from suspicion, but also as payback for Dan's abduction. The bank's papers were now nothing but ash, the thousand dollars were evenly distributed amongst the tribe's Roms, and Mr. Smyth's keys had already been melted down to serve as bullets, silver ware and iron nails by the Romany blacksmith.

As Heck Gidding's face turned red with rage and he took aim at McNally's head, Dan and his new family were already over thirty miles away, driving their separate wagons to all four points of the compass to escape detection.

Chapter Thirty-One

1883

THREE WEEKS LATER, in Mountain Home, Idaho Territory, Dan paid a penny for the latest paper and sat reading it in the mercantile while the supplies he'd ordered for Pedro were being packaged up.

His heart started pounding as he read:

And in other news around the region—The First Security Bank of Laramie was robbed on Friday, June 24th at approximately 2:00 p.m. The bank was stripped of cash, but no customers were injured or killed in the armed exchange. However, two bank employees, the bank's manager, Earl McNally and the head teller, Monty Smyth were found shot to death in the bank's vault, where most of the bank's capital was kept.

Another strange and sad thing happened in the area six days later. A young couple from Missouri, Rhett and Bonnie Kidwell, were found burned to death at their home in the Medicine Bow foothills, about forty-seven miles southeast of Laramie.

The house they had leased burned to the ground while they slept. They leave behind their beloved aunt and uncle, Pete and Maude Holgrum.

May they rest in peace.

OH, my God! Dan thought as the horrible words swam like panicked fish in his mind. Friday was the day after he'd been locked into the bank's vault and later, been rescued by Mr. Smyth and his gypsy friends.

Dan looked up at the mercantile owner and saw that he and his helper were still busy gathering up his order. Then he sat back, closed his eyes and thought back on the last few weeks leading up to today.

Once he and his saviors had gotten back to the gypsy camp from the bank, Pedro sent out some sort of silent but effective alarm. Within minutes of their arrival, the camp was on the move. He recalled Manny coming up to him and saying, "We're going to take your wagon with us, okay, Daniel? It's not painted, you see, and won't be recognized as belonging to the Rom."

Dan hated to disagree right out of the starting gate, but he shook his head and said, "I hate to, Manny. I mean—that sounds good and all, but I already sold it to the Kidwells as a part of the lease to my property. It's theirs now, and they plan on picking it up and taking it home with them tomorrow. I would feel bad about reneging on the deal I made with them…"

"Oh," Manny said, but at that same moment they saw two men lead a horse over to the wagon's traces and start to harness it. Manny took off to stop them, but Dan grabbed his arm and said, "Wait! I'm sorry, but you're right. I guess everything's changed now, and we need that wagon to stay safe, right?"

Manny nodded, but stayed silent, and Dan continued, "As soon as things settle down some, I'll make it up to the Kidwells. It's not like I don't have the money, right? When we get to wherever it is we're going, I'll wire those folks enough money to buy a new wagon."

Manny grinned, "Good thinking, mi amigo. This wagon *will* help us."

Something happened then that startled Dan. While he pitched in to help pack, he saw an assortment of dirty old tarps being stretched over the wagon hoops— affectively covering the gypsies gaily painted tarps that now lay hidden beneath the drab cloth.

Within seconds, the gypsy's caravan resembled any other wagon train and about 2:00 in the dark of the morning, Pedro gathered everyone around him. He said, "You all know what to do, now. I want us to meet in Kuna by the end of next month, ok? That means you lie low, don't visit any towns or fairs, and make haste to our home camp."

One man, a scruffy-looking character who seemed

the most hostile to Dan both now, and last year, when he'd first met them at his and Jake's ranch, growled, "Pedro! You put the Rom in grave peril for this white pup? Why? What is he to us but trouble? Now we won't be able to make the money we need to survive!"

Pedro glared. "That will be enough out of you, Juan. This boy will be working for us from now on and he will triple the amount of money we make at the fairs. You just wait and see!"

Juan screwed up his lips and spat in Pedro's direction, but only after his back was turned. Dan saw several hostile faces staring at him, but he also noticed furious glares directed at Juan for his disrespect toward their leader.

"Now, we must make haste!" Pedro hissed loudly. "I want this caravan long gone before first light!"

This quick escape seemed to Dan like a well-researched maneuver for the gypsies and, just like that, he found himself driving his own wagon west into the arid, southern Wyoming plains. Manny rode by his side, along with two other young men, named Lois and Carlito who sat in back. He was followed by Pedro, his wife Esmeralda, Manny's two sisters, Maria and Conchita, and their old *abuela*, Graciela Nanette.

They had traveled night and day and had made Idaho in an astounding, twelve days. But their luck had run out and so had their supplies. As recompense for his rescue, Dan had volunteered to ride into this little town today and pay for the food and other supplies while the gypsies stayed behind to repair their run-down wagons and tend to their sore-footed horses.

The Rom had tried to give him cash for the needed supplies, but Dan shook his head. "No! All of this is my fault. At least let me pay for the food we need to get to Kuna, okay?" he pleaded.

Pedro had smiled. "Yes, that would be helpful, Daniel. We thank you."

———

DAN SHOOK his head at the memory. Now, he would need to take this newspaper back and report his findings. He felt bad about old Mr. Smyth. He was a brave little guy and had been kind to him. Why did *he* have to die when, apparently, the banks other tellers were safe and sound?

He, frankly, didn't care about that crooked old bank manager, McNally, but it seemed odd that a bunch of gangsters came to rob the bank just one day after he'd been kidnapped within its confines and then, with Smyth's help, had managed to liberate his inheritance.

The newspaper had not named the gang that robbed the bank, but Dan felt a sudden prickly apprehension tickle his spine. Not only had the bank he and Jake used been robbed, and the man who'd helped him escape subsequently killed, the sweet young couple he'd leased his ranch to had died while his house burned to the ground!

He couldn't help but wonder—what were the odds

that three horrible things had happened to the places and people he, himself, was connected to? Although he had no way of knowing if he was imagining things or not, he could almost hear his pa's nemesis, Heck Giddings, rubbing his hands together and cackling in the back of his mind.

Chapter Thirty-Two

UNFORTUNATELY, DAN'S INSTINCTS WERE CORRECT. Heck had been busy and was gaining ground on his ex-partner's son when McNally had intervened and sent the boy fleeing. He wished he could shoot McNally again, just to see the light in his eyes go out... a second time.

A week and a half after Dan had left for the fair, two of his best men, deputy sheriffs, Buzz Williams and Amos Cline had gone to Jake Conrad's homesite deep in the Medicine Bow foothills on a tip from one of his men embedded at the First Security Bank in Laramie.

They had questioned the young couple living at the homestead and found out that Jake himself had passed on but his son, Daniel, had leased them his property and planned on going out into the world to see what he could find. After getting as much information on the situation as they could, the deputies had snuck back later and torched the house with the man and woman still sleeping inside.

Heck was pleased, thinking, *one less thread snipped for good.* He had been searching for the traitor, Jake Conrad for so long it had become more than a habit… it was a compulsion to rectify a wrong. *Why*, he had thought more than once, *I saved that kid from himself, uplifted him from a booze-addled tramp, into a first-rate pistol man and outlaw. I fed him, and taught him and made him into something substantial, instead of the fly-speck he was before he joined my gang!*

For years after Jake's disappearance, Hector had felt a mixture of rage and sorrow. He couldn't get past the man's betrayal—the feeling that all his love and affection had been chewed up and then spat back in his face. So, he had begun his search for Jake Conrad and had vowed to find and kill the man if it was the last thing he ever did.

The rejection still stung, even seven years later, and now his search had found fruit… or had that fruit died on the vine? Apparently, Jake Conrad was dead now, and despite his vow to end the man, Heck felt Jake's passing and knew it had opened new wounds.

Then, Brian Talbot, his embedded bank teller told him that Jake had strolled into the First Security Bank last summer and asked for help with his estate. He had requested Monty Smyth's assistance, but Brian's desk was close enough to Smyth's that he could hear almost every word spoken, in between customers.

It seemed as if Jake knew his days were numbered

and he had money and property he wanted signed over to his son. *Son! What son?* Heck wondered. The only son Heck knew of was a baby boy who had died, along with his mother-which was the reason Jake had set out to drink himself to death before Heck had found him and given him a whole new purpose in life.

Brian had gone on to say that Jake told Smyth that he'd found the boy wandering around the plains of northern Colorado after a wagon train robbery, seven years earlier and he had taken the boy in as a foster son. These words, of course, sent a chill up Hack's spine, and he'd sat himself down and done a little arithmetic in his head.

Seven years ago! The exact same time Jake had come up missing after one of the gangs many heists in the Colorado Territory. That would mean, if he was figuring correctly and he was pretty sure his calculations were accurate, the boy had been a part of that train and had somehow escaped—with Jake's help.

Heck's blood ran cold at the thought. That would mean, after all these years, there was a living witness to his crimes! And that would not do, not at all.

Hector Gidding's gang had long since been dismantled and most of the original members were gone; either killed and buried, or like him, hidden in plain sight, disguised behind the veneer of respectability with new names, occupations, and meticulous, fictional histories.

Heck had realized, even as a small boy, that money and entitlement was not handed out fairly. You either inherited quality, or you somehow lucked into it, *or* you fought for it, tooth and nail. He was born to a drunken, abusive miner father and a barroom-scull. When he wasn't ducking his father's furious fists; he'd learned to steal, connive and finally, survive his way into early adulthood, where he found steady work for the many notorious outlaw gangs in the southern colony-states.

He'd become adept at thievery, embezzlement, extortion and murder and before too long, he was the boss of his own outfit. But being the leader of a band of ruthless cutthroats was not his aim and never had been. What he longed for was wealth, power and esteem.

He wanted to wear fine suits, and have a perfectly coiffed, heavily perfumed woman on one arm and a respectable, starchy wife on the other. He wanted to clench a fine Havana cigar in his teeth and command the respect of his peers—other men like him; who wielded power as easily as a quirt in one hand and made, or broke kings as easily as breathing air.

And now, in his forty-seventh year, he was close to achieving his ambitions. It had taken time, sacrifice, patience, and sheer cold-blooded willpower but now he had a fine mansion on top of a hill, a wealthy wife, and two discreet but beautiful prostitutes hanging on his arm whenever he stepped out in public.

Not only that, but he was currently in close competition with David Koats—a South Carolina blue blood —for the position of governor for the territory of

Wyoming. The former governor, an oldster by the name of Morris Whitham, had died of heart failure shortly after his inauguration, leaving the elected position open to newcomers.

He had no political clout in the territory of Wyoming, but he did have a lot of money, enough capital to buy the position if he cared to—which he did. He wanted no part of running the state—he would hire people to do that job—but he craved the power that came with that position like a cat craved cream.

Everything was lining up beautifully, but now there was a fly in the ointment... Jake Conrad's adopted son, Dan. Giddings gritted his teeth in frustration. He was so close and now a witness to his past crimes had suddenly popped up—a witness who could not only foil his plans but get him hanged!

Well, he thought, *it's high time to track that pup down once and for all!*

Chapter Thirty-Three

THE ONE THING DAN ACCOMPLISHED WHILE TRAVELING with the gypsies to Idaho was proof that he could, indeed, shoot. At first, he spent most of his spare time shooting critters for their cook pots. But eventually, once Pedro began to feel that the threat of being tracked down by lawmen from Laramie had passed, he asked Dan to demonstrate his pistol work.

Manny, Louis, and Carlito set up wood-bark targets at 50 feet, 75 feet, and 100 feet as Dan stood alone, his heart suddenly thudding with nerves. Jake had always told him not to get too puffed up... that Dan had a long way to go before he could call himself a "Pistol-Man." Now, his pa's words echoed in his mind.

What if he was just a so-so shootist? What if his skills were only magnified in his head, and Jake was just being polite on those rare occasions he went so far as to approve Dan's efforts? Manny's excited voice pierced his thoughts.

"Daniel!' he shouted. "Go ahead and show mi Papá what you can do!"

Manny had never seen Dan shoot, but the young man had so much blind faith in his abilities, Dan shuddered with dread. He blushed but remembered Juan's doubt and ridicule and knew that even now, the gypsy's goodwill rested on his ability to make an impression with his guns. He saw Pedro's wife and two daughters scramble out the back of their schooner and blushed again.

Night after night while traveling north and west into Idaho territory, he had sat by his fire and watched as the Amaya sisters practiced their dance routines. And recently, Dan had found his eyes resting with longing on Manny's older sister, Maria. He found her to be so beautiful, so sensuous, so... desirable he could hardly sleep at night.

Her hair was as dark and shiny as a raven's wing, her lips as red as strawberries and her eyes as deep and dark as a starlit mountain pool. But, she was almost twenty-years-old, three years older than he was, and he felt like a rank calf, bawling after the moon.

For the first time in his life, he felt his boyish needs and desires replaced by something far more mature, and almost irresistible. He had, once or twice felt her dark eyes upon him and saw her white teeth flash in amusement, but she always left quickly and kept her distance whenever he joined her family for dinner.

Which was just as well, he thought with a sigh. Manny had spoken often and with pride of his family and had said that Maria was promised to one of the other Rom's oldest sons—a fine young man named Rafe who was, apparently, good at whatever he did; strong as an ox, fleet as a deer and so on and so forth.

Dan rolled his eyes. He had not seen or met this paragon, but he was already sick of hearing about Rafe's daring exploits. He was jealous, plain and simple, and wished he were bigger, badder, stronger—anything it took to gain Maria's admiration.

Taking a deep, calming breath, Dan realized that what he was attempting to do right now, might just do the trick and he turned sideways a bit, as his pa had taught him, took aim and put a bullet smack-dab in the middle of the first target. Then, he stepped to the left slightly and did the same thing on the next target and, after a moment's hesitation, drilled a hole in the center of the last, 100-foot target, shattering the flat bark into chaff.

Manny, Louis and Carlito whooped with joy and Pedro nodded in approval, but when Dan looked past the older man's shoulder to see Maria's reaction, he was disappointed to find that she was not watching him at all. Instead, she and her little sister Conchita were carrying a basket of laundry down to a nearby creek.

Old Granny Nanette had climbed down from her wagon, though, and she clapped her hands and took a little jump in the air like a young girl. Then, as Dan watched she faltered and her face grew pale. Pedro reached over and grasped her arm, obviously concerned, and Dan holstered his pistol and ran up to them saying, "Oh, Granny Nanette! Did my gun scare you? I'm so sorry..."

But the old woman sat still on the log she'd been led to and all Dan could see was the white of her eyes. Thoroughly frightened, he watched as her daughter-in-law, Esmeralda, wrote the words Granny was muttering down in a paper notebook. The first thing Dan thought was, *Look at that paper! That old book must be worth a fortune!*

Paper products were very expensive—a true luxury out here on the plains and seeing the almost priceless gilt paper notebook and equally expensive ink quill in Esmeralda's hands was a shock. But then, he heard his name being muttered as the old woman shuddered and groaned as if beset with a fit.

She mumbled a bunch of words in a foreign language and then she seemed to recover a bit and fell against her son with a sigh. Pedro stroked his mother's arm and asked his wife to lead Nanette back to the wagon for a nice nap. Esmeralda nodded, and helped old granny to her feet. Before walking away, she looked up at Dan who stood still as a statue. Then she took a step and reached up to pat his cheek. She said, "You are not quite ready yet, son, but keep on working at it. You'll need to be as good as good gets to face what's coming..." Then she staggered again and allowed her daughter-in-law to lead her away to the wagon.

Dan stood swaying in shock. *It was Jake...* he thought. *My pa was just speaking to me from the grave!*

Old Granny's voice had roughened, and momentarily taken on Jake's drawl, and Dan knew that somehow, abuela Nanette had just channeled Jake's spirit in order to warn him of an impending threat.

His mouth dropped, and Pedro gazed up at him with pity. "Mi Mama is rarely wrong, you know. When she has her little fits, the Rom listen for she has the gift of foresight. So, you are hired, okay? You are very good... I saw this with my own eyes. But you must be better. Granny has said so. You must be better, for all our sakes."

Chapter Thirty-Four

So, Dan practiced and practiced some more until his old callouses broke open, blistered up and grew bigger and tougher than ever. He had wanted more gunpowder before he was forced to flee Laramie, but since he'd had been pretty slack at re-loading his bullet casings over the last few weeks, he still had enough powder left to grow as sharp with his targets as he ever was.

He practiced night and day and made sure to give his left hand as thorough a work-out as his right. This was hard for him, although his pa had insisted he learn. The process was the same, as well as the bullets and his guns, but it seemed as if changing hands threw his whole outlook off—as if he needed to train his eyes, his brain and his heart to go counter-clockwise. He was certainly slower shooting left-hand and he knew that he needed to improve his speed if he and his friends were going to survive a combat situation. Jake had once told him that he, himself, was ambidextrous... a big, fancy word for being both right-and-left-handed. Shooting left-hand had come naturally to Jake but Dan struggled.

Manny, Louis and Carlito were also learning to shoot. Only Manuel had ever handled a firearm, and that was his Papá's rifle. The other boys only knew knife work, not guns and their incompetence was spectacular. After two dangerous near-misses during practice, (one time, Louise had turned around with Dan's pistol and accidentally blew Manny's hat off his head, and once he had almost blown his own toes off!) Dan finally asked Louis to keep working on his knife skills (which were outstanding) and perhaps, instead of learning to shoot, just help his friends with reloading their bullets.

He didn't want to hurt the other boy's feeling, but Louis was a menace with a gun, and he seemed to know it. Accepting Dan's suggestion with good grace he said, "¡Si. Yo so muy malo... bad with pistoles!" Grinning, he bent over and picked up a handful of spent cartridges from the ground and sat off to the side with a small bucket of powder while the other boys practiced.

It took another three days to reach Kuna. They could have made better time, but no one seemed to be chasing them right now, and Pedro decided to spare the horses and wagons until they reached the gypsy's main camp. At about three in the afternoon, Pedro and his wagons rolled into a large grassy meadow and Dan saw about fifty brightly painted wagons gathered together along a small river. He saw a half a dozen small cook fires scattered throughout the encampment and could even hear music ringing out in the distance.

Early July heat waves rose in undulating patterns throughout the valley and Dan could felt sweat trickling down his neck and back. He was nervous and knew that he needed to prove himself again with these new gypsies, but at least he felt confident that his shooting skills would probably earn him a place amongst the Rom. Seeing the excited exclamations and huge smiles directed their way as they pulled into camp, Dan felt almost at home.

He did not notice a pair of dark, smoldering eyes that watched his approach from behind one of the wagons. Juan had not forgiven Dan, or Pedro, for making him look the fool in front of his peers. And he swore, on the blessed Virgin's honor, that he would exact his revenge on that stupid pup. Although Juan knew it might take time and a certain amount of cunning, he would drive that white boy away from the Rom—for good.

———

HECK GIDDINGS SAT BACK in his office chair and scowled at one of his henchmen, a private detective named, Travis Worley. Worley was talking a mile a minute, acutely aware that his boss was neither pleased nor impressed with the news he'd brought about the boy and his last known whereabouts.

"Honestly, sir, no one has seen hide nor hair of that kid since he escaped from the bank that night!" he repeated.

Heck loosened his starchy collar and pulled the string tie away from his sweating neck. Cheyenne was suffering under the same heat spell as southern Idaho, and Heck glanced up at the ceiling fan that was still set to low and barely moving the hot air around the room. He yearned to call one of his lackeys in to fix the fan, but the conversation was too sensitive for prying ears.

"Tell me again… who did you talk to?" he asked.

Worley shrugged. "Well, a bunch of shop-owners, the wait staff at the two hotels in town, and the same at the four cafes. No one saw Dan Monroe. I did talk with the owner of the only gunsmith in town, and he knew both Jake Conrad and the kid, but he told me he never saw either one of them this year."

Heck frowned. "Wasn't there a pretty big fair that same week? Did you talk to any of those vendors?"

Worley shook his head. "Nah, by the time me and Tom got there, the Rondo was over and most of the vendors had already moved on—you know those folks follow the circuit." Worley scratched his head and his eyes got a far-away look as though an idea had suddenly occurred to him.

"What?" Heck urged.

Worley shook his head and shrugged. "Not sure. I just remembered one of those folks sayin' it was a strange year this time around. You know, the gypsies are usually a big draw, but they didn't show up until the rondo was almost over, and then they up and left in the middle of the night—just one night after they pulled in. Apparently, they never do that, and there were still a few days left of the Rondo," he paused and pulled a small notebook out of his pant's pocket. Flipping a few pages, he studied his notes, pulled his hair this way and that, and his eyes got big.

"What, dammit?" Heck was going crazy watching his hired detective scratch his head like a monkey.

Worley grinned. "I think I just found a clue or, at least, a pretty big coincidence."

"Spill it, damn you," the governor hissed.

"The gypsies took off in the middle of the same night your boy, Dan Monroe, escaped. What are the odds of that happening?" Worley grinned.

Chapter Thirty-Five

THREE OR FOUR REGULARLY SCHEDULED FAIRS HAD BEEN skipped because of their hasty escape from Laramie, and the gypsies, although sympathetic toward the young white boy in their midst were worried about their ability to survive the coming winter with so little money in their coffers.

Two days after their arrival at the base camp in Idaho, Pedro asked Dan to join him for the Rom's weekly meeting. Heart pounding with nervous apprehension, Dan followed Pedro to a large cook fire and saw about twenty men gathered together in a circle around the flames. Even as they approached, Dan could hear Juan complaining about his presence at the gypsy's camp.

"And, Pedro never even took a vote, which you know is the normal thing to do!" he exclaimed as Pedro and Dan sat down on two stumps of wood. Dan's heart sank. He didn't even know these men yet and already Juan was besmirching his character!

But Pedro said, "Juan. You hated this boy before he even joined us. You hate heem because he is white, and he had the courage to challenge the men who were hurting my son last summer, while you hid behind the wagons in camp and shivered with fear!" Pedro screwed up his lips and spat. "Bah! ¡*Hijo de puta!*"

Juan took a menacing step forward as if to fight but an old man with long white braids, held his hand in the air. "Stop this, Juan… and you too, Pedro."

Pedro, who was shaking with rage, stared at Juan for a moment and then sat back down on his stump. He whispered to Dan, "That is Don Domingo, our leader." Grumbling, Juan walked away behind the seated men and glared at Dan. Dan gazed back and saw that the older man was fingering the hilt of a savage-looking machete at his belt. He wanted to feel the comforting grip of his own guns, but Pedro had asked Dan to stow his weapons while staying with the Rom.

The old man took a bag of tobacco out of his shirt pocket and rolled a cigarette. Lighting up, he gazed across the low-burning fire toward Pedro, and said, "It is true that mingling with the whites usually brings trouble to our people…"

Pedro nodded silently and stood to speak but the older man was not finished yet. He took a long drag off his cigarette and continued. "I have heard something of your plans, old friend. Please explain to me now what you want us to do for capital, and how this gringo fits into your scheme."

So, Pedro went about explaining his ideas of turning the gypsies more passive way of making a living into a show; featuring the gypsies knife skills, and Daniel's skill with guns in addition to their usual fortune telling, horse racing and dance routines. He added, "And... many of our women make wonderful soups, stews and pastries; recipes that come straight from the 'Old World.' I think we should also sell food to the customers."

Dom Domingo nodded thoughtfully and gazed into the fire while the men gathered around the fire murmured to each other and glanced in Dan's direction. Dan noted that most of the men seemed kindly disposed to the idea.

Domingo looked up, and said, "What of this one's family, eh? How do *they* feel about him joining the gypsies? The last thing we need is an angry *Papá* shaking us down for money or going to the sheriffs with kidnapping charges."

Pedro shrugged. "Sí, you are right but this one has no family. He is alone in this world."

Although Dan knew Pedro's words were simply the truth, for some reason his chest was suddenly heavy with sorrow. He was an orphan, for sure, and heavily dependent upon Pedro's support. Overcome with emotion, he blinked back the tears that threatened his composure, and sat up straight with as much dignity as he could muster. He gazed at Dom Domingo with calm eyes although he missed Jake so much, right now, it hurt.

Domingo studied the boy's face and saw his emotional struggle. "Is this true, Daniel? Do you have no family?" The old man's voice was firm but kind.

Daniel replied, "Yes, sir. My pa died last spring, and there's no one else… except for my friends here."

"And, do you shoot as well as my friend Pedro says?" Domingo asked.

"Yessir! My pa taught me. I think I would make you proud if you let me join the show."

Domingo looked down at the fire again, as the cigarette in his right hand smoldered into ash. The other men looked back and forth between their leader and the boy and whispered their opinions in each other's ears.

Finally, Domingo said, "Pedro, I like your idea. I think it would help our people to diversify. I never saw that show you and the others did, but the old, sly ways of the Rom are coming to an end. There are too many of us to feed and care for properly without more cash in our coffers."

He looked Dan up and down, adding, "I will allow you to participate, Daniel. But, if you bring trouble down on the Rom, you will be asked to leave, ¿sí?"

Daniel smiled and nodded, but couldn't help but think, *there is already trouble on my heels! Should I make that clear now, or wait and see—and hope against hope that he had left his troubles far behind in Wyoming?*

The decision was snatched away from him, though,

as Juan muscled his way to the front of the crowd. "This boy *is* trouble, Dom Domingo! It was because of heem we had to flee the fair in Wyoming! Surely, Pedro explained this to you, already?" His dark eyes gleamed with challenge as Pedro stood up from the stump he sat on.

"Of course, Dom Domingo knows what happened, Juan," he snapped. "What do you take me for? I not only talked to our Rom about what happened to Daniel at that bank, I also explained our part in taking money from the vault. The money we stole is already in his hands and it will be spread evenly amongst us... or, did you think I would keep it for myself?" Pedro was watching Juan carefully and so was Dom Domingo.

Dan wasn't too worldly, but even he could see the air leave Juan's body and his shoulders slump. Apparently, he thought he held some sort of trump card against Pedro. But now, knowing that Domingo knew exactly what had happened in Laramie, he left Juan with no ammunition with which to turn the tide against Pedro and his plans. Frustrated, he threw one hand into the air, made an obscene gesture and left the gathering in a huff.

Domingo spoke, "It is getting late now, but tomorrow we'll gather again and make plans for our new future in... how do they call it? Show Business?"

Chapter Thirty-Six

TWO AND A HALF WEEKS LATER, DAN AND THE ROMANI were debuting their new show in Kuna on the western outskirts of Boise. The first day had set the precedent for the rest of the tour, and now their new show was a success. The usual crowd of about thirty men and women had come to get their fortunes told or to watch the exotic dancers and place bets on the Gypsy horse races.

But, once the usual entertainment was concluded, the customers were in for an unexpected treat. All of them began to smell the fragrance of shish kebab, curry, fried sweet corn and honeyed cakes as the Romany women brought their specialty dishes out to a series of long tables. Samples to go were priced to sell, but all the customers were allowed a small taste of the gypsy's fare. Twenty minutes after the food was brought out, it was sold, and the Rom were dumbstruck at the unaccustomed wealth they were able to spirit away.

Juan, who was generally considered to be a pain in the rump, was possessed of a fine, deep voice and he had been picked to be the Rom's mouthpiece. Before the crowd had a chance to trickle off after the food was served, he stepped up on a wooden box and announced, "Ladies and Gents—we are pleased to present, Daniel the Two-Shooter! Please, step up to the line and observe the fastest gun West of the Missouri River!

Dan hated his new moniker but understood the need to dramatize his position as much as possible. Still, he thought uncomfortably, what good did that kind of boast do you, but challenge every Tom, Dick and Harry to disprove your claim to fame?

He took a deep breath, bowed to the two dozen or so spectators that had wandered over to eat their goodies and watch, and turned to face several brightly colored, human-shaped targets set up in the distance. Without further ado, he drilled each of the targets— one in the head, one for each shoulder, bullets for each imaginary hipbone, a bullet per leg and one for the heart.

Boom! Boom-boom, Boom-boom, Boom-boom! Boom! At once, the men watching Dan's display stopped eating and simply stared at the boy with shock. The women in the crowd, sensing that something unusual was happening with the young man, turned to stare as Dan did the same thing over again just as quickly but now with his left hand.

"By God, that kid really *can* shoot!" one old-timer muttered, and another man answered, "I'm bettin' he's just a one-trick pony..." Suddenly, the Romany men were standing in amongst the crowd with their hats held out, asking if the fine gentlemen were willing to place a bet on the kid's prowess.

An hour later, the men and women in the crowd were relieved of much of their spare change and Dan Monroe had gained a reputation. It seemed to the dazzled crowd that the boy could shoot at anything, whether still or moving, right or left-handed and without breaking a sweat! They had unexpectedly been treated to a display of gunmanship the like of which they'd never seen before and would likely never see again.

Dan, who knew his pa was a gifted pistol man, was genuinely unaware of his own talent and how far he'd come since he'd first started training. Jake, although loving in his own way, had relied on criticism rather than compliments to hone Dan's skills, so now the young man focused on his own perceived lack of speed and despaired over his one miss—a lightweight wooden bird that had been launched into the tall branches of a tree rather than out in the open. He had actually winged the thing, but it was difficult to shatter it, as ordered, when it was hidden in amongst the tree's leaves.

Pedro was grinning from ear to ear. Everyone in the

crowd had stayed to watch the extended show and had eventually wandered over to the throwing wheel to watch Manny and his friends throw their knives at the wheel and the young girls who were tied, wrists and feet, to the spinning device while sharp knives etched their outlines.

The Romany women circulated through the crowds with their traditional, heavy layered skirts serving Baklava and tin cups of cheap red wine for a penny a piece, and the smaller gypsy children were dancing and tumbling through the audience and doing a fine job with some light pick-pocket work. *Not too much*, they'd been cautioned, and *nothing too costly*, but still, a few pennies here and there was the cost the *gadje* must pay to mingle with the Rom.

His idea was a resounding success, and glancing behind him where Dom Domingo sat in front of his wagon smoking a cigarette, Pedro saw the old man smile and wink in approval.

They were scheduled to stay in that spot for a week; and after the first day, the crowds swelled, and swelled some more until the town's sheriffs and deputies were called in to keep order. Dan kept up the good work and many a young miss fell in love with the scarred but beautiful blue-eyed boy who stood as still and somber as a statue as he blew every target in front of him to smithereens.

The Romany boys had their fair-share of admirers as well, and every young buck in the area was completely smitten by the Gypsy dancers, and the girls who spent their days pinned to the deadly knife wheels. Every night, the Rom males needed to go into town for more supplies for the food they were serving during the show, and the old grannies were growing weary of telling the same fortunes over and over again.

Two days before they were scheduled to end the performances and move on, Dan, Manny and a bunch of other boys set out to the next town on their list, which was the town of Nampa. As they rode into town they were met by an unofficial but exuberant crowd of kids and old men, who had already heard of them and promised to pin up and display their hand-written notices and promised to advertise their coming to one and all.

Dan was flabbergasted and as excited as Manny, who was not only proud of his Papá for coming up with the idea in the first place, but at how well the show was doing and the gypsies in general now that their coffers were starting to overflow.

The boys didn't realize, yet, that fame almost always came at a cost, and that other eyes were now watching their success with alarm and greed.

Chapter Thirty-Seven

ONE OF THE PEOPLE WHO WATCHED DAN MONROE WITH alarm was his old friend, Long Knife. He, his wife and child and his few remaining tribe members had come to the Boise area because they did not want to be rounded up and driven back to one of the newly-formed reservations that had sprung up like mushrooms since the Battle of the Little Bighorn.

After saying goodbye to Jake and Daniel and leaving southern Wyoming, Long Knife and his people found themselves on the run nine days out of ten, and the buffalo which used to be so plentiful in Wyoming and northern Colorado had disappeared. Vast herds of the shaggy beasts could be found laid out dead and stinking for miles on end. What had shocked Knife the most was that most of the animals had not been killed for meat, but for their hides, and he simply couldn't fathom why nature's plenty had been disregarded in that way—especially since his own small band of rene-gades was always on the verge of starvation.

Having met up with other friendly bands of refugee Indians, Knife had learned that unlike the southern plains, buffalo were still plentiful up north in Idaho, Montana, and Canada. Also, most of the military troops who had stayed on after the Greasy Grass War had moved south, searching for Sitting Bull and his many generals.

Knife had stopped by the Medicine Bow to visit Jake and Daniel but found the house and nearby barn burnt to the ground. Some of the animals—mainly a few head of cattle and sheep, had died from lack of water and starvation, but the mules, goats and most of the horses had broken down the fence and made their escape.

Knife, feeling a keen sense of loss, had stared at the devastation of his uncle's homestead and mourned. He understood that life was a cheap commodity these days, for white folks as well as his own kind, but still—his uncle had always seemed eternal to him and the boy he'd adopted and raised had that same fierce fire in his young eyes. It was almost inconceivable that both Jake and Dan were now dead.

So, he and what remained of his people moved north to where the buffalo still thrived, and to where he thought another bigger, stronger tribe of Cheyenne flourished. He hoped that they would welcome his people as their own—many of them were his own cousins after all, and he felt hopeful; especially since there were now more woman and children in his band than fighting braves, which was always a good bargaining chip for the plains Indians.

They had camped outside of one of Fort Hall, Idaho Territory, to trade what little they possessed—buffalo hides, a few fine pieces of traditional jewelry and some beautiful beaded leather shirts, skirts and leggings for food and maybe a little whiskey for their witch doctor.

He hated being so close to white people now. He was the chief of his tribe and although quite young-as chiefs went—he was prepared to fight to the death to keep his band safe from harm. Still, he was amazed at how he and his tribe were ignored by the many people, horses and wagons driving by their small encampment. And there really was a lot of foot and wagon traffic on this hot, dusty morning.

He stood by himself in front of his tribes three tipis and could catch snatches of conversation as the wagons rumbled past. "Heard he's the fastest gun in the west..." one man called out to a man in another wagon, and a few minutes later, "He ain't but a kid, ya know... bet he could take on Billy the Kid, push came to shove..."

"Billy the Kid? Why he's dead and buried years ago!" The other man cackled.

"Wahl, you know what I mean, anyway. Fast as greased lightning is what I heard..." the first man insisted.

A fast gun, and only a kid? Knife heard the words and couldn't help but wonder. He honestly couldn't believe how much young Daniel had improved with his uncle's tutelage. Remembering Daniel's skinny arms and how he'd struggled with his first bow, and then seeing the authority with which he handled both his bow and Jake's pistols only five years later, Knife's heart began to thunder in his chest. Could it be?

Deciding abruptly to go and see for himself, he walked to his tipi and donned a leather over-shirt and an old hat he'd found on the trail. He told his wife he would be back soon, kissed his son and headed down the road to see if Jake and Daniel had gone into pistol work for a living.

———

UNFORTUNATELY, another pair of cool gray eyes watched Daniel as well. These eyes belonged to one of Heck Gidding's henchmen: a gun-toter by the name of Tom Blackwell.

Blackwell had decided to make himself scarce after he saw Gidding's blow Earl McNally's head off at the bank in Laramie. Although there was no love lost between himself and McNally, Tom thought Gidding's actions were entirely un-called for.

Lord knew, he had taken his fair share of Gidding's illegitimate wealth on the sly and wanted no part of the man's revenge. *Plus, for Pete's sake*, he thought, resentfully, *Heck himself had ordered the seizure of that stupid kid... just because Dan had managed to get away was no reason to put an end to McNally's worthless existence, was it?*

Tom had been sent to look for Daniel Monroe, along with most of Heck's other gun fighters, and now he stood staring at the kid with his mouth turned down in shock and dismay. *Why, no wonder that little scamp got the drop on McNally!*, he thought, uneasily.

The kid was as familiar to Tom as the back of his hand. He had kept a close eye on him as McNally led him into the vault portion of the bank. He sure didn't look or act like that shy and raggedy boy he'd seen in the bank that day, though. That boy had shuffled along in line looking scairt and bewildered. He was dressed in dirty skins, an old slouch hat and hand-stitched moccasins. Tom had been as shocked as anyone to learn that Dan had two guns on each hip under that grimy-looking duster.

The boy in front of him now wore new Levi Strauss jeans, beautiful square-toed, knee-high cowboy boots, a snowy white shirt and a brightly embroidered vest. An expensive looking gray Stetson complimented his long black hair, and his two pistols were polished and clean.

And boy, could he shoot! Tom had made a living with his pistol work, but he knew for a fact that he couldn't hold a candle to Daniel Monroe's guns and without a *lot* of help, he would die trying. There was a $500-dollar reward on offer to the first man who located Jake Conrad's son, and $1,000 dollars to the man who brought Monroe in dead. Thinking about it for a minute or two, Tom decided to spare his own hide and catch a train to Laramie and Heck Giddings hell bent for leather with his information, rather than try to bring the youngster in on his own.

Safer that way, he nodded to himself, *and hey, $500 bucks is still a pretty good grubstake.*

Chapter Thirty-Eight

As Tom Black rode his horse into town to visit the train depot and buy a ticket to Laramie, Dan got the happiest shock of his young life. Just as his part of the show ended, and most of the crowd had wandered off to watch the knife wheels and buy the Gypsies fare, he saw an Indian man watching him from the back of the crowd.

Dan stared and then broke into a wide grin. Grabbing his hat, he tossed it high in the air and hollered, "Knife! Is that you?" He broke into a run, galloped up to where Long Knife stood, and launched himself at the Indian man with his arms opened wide.

Giving Knife a bear hug, Dan exclaimed, "Wow, Knife! I thought I'd never see you again! Whatcha doin' here?"

Long Knife tolerated the boy's affection for a few moments and then gently pushed him back to gaze up into his eyes. (At six-feet, Daniel Monroe was already taller than Knife would ever be.) "I heard about a fast shooter, Daniel. Not finding you or my uncle at home in the Medicine Bow, we came here to find better hunting, and now I find you. But where is Jake?" Knife looked past Dan's shoulder as if expecting his uncle to walk up at any moment.

Dan could go for days and even weeks without weeping over Jake's passing, but the slightest mention of his beloved Pa could set him off. This time was no exception. Dan went from shouts of joy to tears of sorrow in the blink of an eye as he informed Long Knife of Jake's illness and passing over this early spring.

The young Indian was deeply saddened, but he admonished Dan, "A warrior feels the pain of those he leaves behind, Daniel. Please do not mourn so—do you want my uncle to suffer for your loss?"

Dan's eyes got big as he wiped his face dry. He remembered his pa talking about the Indian way of viewing life and death and he felt shame at how he had carried on. He knew Jake would be mad at him for his "sissy" ways, and vowed to mourn no longer (at least, publicly).

He nodded at his old friend and said, "Yes Knife. You're right about that. I just miss him sometimes."

Knife smiled and said, "As do I, Young Wolverine… as do I."

Dan stared at Long Knife. "Wolverine?" He fingered the faint white lines on his cheek and remembered his

The Pistol Man's Apprentice

battle with the creature that had maimed him. "Why do you call me that?"

"It is what all the people call you, Daniel. Didn't Jake tell you this?" Knife answered.

Dan shook his head. "No, he didn't." He grinned, adding, "Probably thought a nice handle like that would go to my head!"

Knife sobered. "Yes, knowing my uncle, he wouldn't want you to grow prideful in your skills." Looking around, he said, "You do pistol work for the Travelers now?"

Dan nodded. "Yes, Jake warned me to leave the Medicine Bow as quick as possible after he was gone. He was worried about his old boss, Heck Giddings, coming after me. I don't know about him, I hear he's runnin' for governor of Wyoming now, but a crooked banker in Laramie tried to kidnap me and take all my inheritance before I met up with a gypsy friend of mine who saved me and offered me a job for this new show they got going on." He sighed. "I miss the farm though... Hopefully, I can go back someday, and rebuild."

Long Knife frowned at him for a second and said, "So, you heard??"

Dan felt his heart sink when he asked, "About the farm and the folks I leased it to burning up? Yeah, I read about it in the newspaper."

Then Knife said, "Please, tell me about what happened at the bank, Daniel."

Dan answered, "Wahl, Jake left me the deed to the

homestead and about two thousand dollars in cash. He wanted me to leave the area, remember? So, I went to the fair and then walked to the bank to pull my money out. That's when the bank manager, a man named McNally, led me to the back of the bank and then locked me inside the vault. I think he was going to rob me but wanted all the customers out of the bank first.

I would probably still be there—or dead and buried —if it wasn't for my gypsy friends. Once they realized I was missing, they came and got me outta there, before that rotten bank man took all my cash..." He paused as Long Knife started and shook his head in alarm.

"What is it, Knife?" he asked his friend.

Knife closed his eyes for a moment and then said, "Jake came to the council meeting the night you and he first arrived in our camp. Do you remember that?"

Looking back, Dan nodded and remembered that he was so tired, sore and grief-stricken at the time, the Indians and what happened after he and Jake arrived was nothing but a colorful blur in his mind's eye. He did recall Jake telling him to get some sleep, though, while he went to talk to the village elders. "I remember..." he answered, and Knife continued.

"Jake talked about that man, Heck Giddings, and his many lieutenants, and how he had made his escape from them but felt honor-bound to save you from the outlaws, before taking shelter with us. He wanted us to know that he and you were being hunted, and to give us fair warning that there might be a fight."

He fell silent for a moment and Dan wanted to know more, but then Knife roused himself and said, "Daniel, do you remember how mighty we were then? We had over forty tipis, and almost a hundred men, women and children—we had over thirty fighting braves! Do you remember?"

Knife sounded so forlorn, Dan's throat tightened, and he had to swallow back his emotions. He put his hand on Knife's right arm and murmured, "Yes, Long Knife. I remember well."

Knife sat up straight, and pride glittered in his deep-set brown eyes. "Well," he continued. "we were not worried about a few bandits—we knew that together we would defeat them all. And, it turned out that they did not come looking for Jake after-all, so you two were able to make a life in the Medicine Bow."

Dan and Knife sat still for a moment or two, recalling those days long past and then Knife said, "The reason I mention this, Daniel, is because Jake told us the names of the men who served Giddings. Most I have forgotten, but I know the name McNally... he was one of that bandit's top lieutenants."

Dan sat and stared at his old friend with shock. "Do you mean to say that it was really Heck Giddings who had a hold of me that day?"

Knife nodded, and said, "I may be wrong, but I think it's no surprise that a trusted ally would try to seize you for his boss."

Dan seethed. *I was so close!*, he mourned. *All I had to*

do was wait for Giddings to show up, and I would have had my pa's enemy in my sights! But I'm so dumb, I couldn't put two and two together, and I lost my best chance of killing him!

Chapter Thirty-Nine

HECK GIDDINGS SAT IN HIS STUDY AND STUDIED THE dark eyed man in front of him and felt a sort of loathing. He knew that Tom Black, along with Earl McNally had been robbing him blind for the last five years and he also thought that Black would turn on a dime if he thought it might profit him. He was a witness to the cold-blooded murder of McNally and the legitimate bank teller, Monty Smyth. and Giddings now felt that Black was a loose thread that would be better off clipped than allowed to unravel his plans.

For now, though, Black had good news. "Big as day and bold as brass, Boss. Kid's doing some sharp-shooting for a band of Gyps in Kuna just outside of Boise. You want me and a few other men to go after him?"

Giddings stared at him with mocking eyes. "What I wanna know is why you had to high-tail it back here to tell me about it and fetch more hands when you just as easily could have done the job yourself. I would rather see Dan Monroe dead and stretched out over a pack saddle than spend the time and resources running him down 'cause you were too chicken to do it on your own!"

Black's cheeks turned red and he found himself, not for the first time, wanting to drill Gidding's fat, smug face full of holes. Still, he wasn't ready to buck the man yet. Plus, he knew that this big house was filled to the brim with Heck's loyal followers and figured he would follow Giddings straight to hell, shortly after he pulled the trigger.

So, he swallowed his pride and said, "Boss, sorry, but there's a good reason those Gyps hired that kid. He's excellent with those guns of his... one of the fastest I've ever seen, and I seen a lot. I just thought it would be better to send a crew, than have that sprout gun us down, one by one."

Giddings *had* heard about the boy's prowess and thought, *leave it to Jake to teach the boy how to handle a pistol. Jake was, after all, one of the best pistol men I've ever seen.*

Deciding to cut Black a little slack, for now, Giddings nodded and said, "You are right, I guess. The sooner we get rid of that kid, the better. Might as well send a team to finish the task. So, gather up about five of our best shooters..." he paused for a moment and frowned, "Just remember, there are more ways than a bullet to close a busy mouth for good. Gunplay is a noisy business, so try to stop him without making a scene. I don't care what you boys do—hell, put him in a sack and drown him like a kitten, it don't matter, just get the job done."

———

DAN AND KNIFE visited a few more minutes and then Manny and his father walked over to where they sat on the ground talking. Both father and son were gazing at Long Knife with keen eyes.

"¡Hola!" Pedro said with a broad smile. "Daniel, we came to tell you to grab something to eat quick before it is all gone." Glancing at Knife, he asked, "Who is your freend?"

Dan, remembering his manners, said, "Oh, sorry... Mr. Amaya—Manny, this is my old friend, Long Knife. He is Cheyenne and is... was my pa's nephew." Turning to Knife, he introduced his gypsy friends, and Knife gave a slight, but respectful dip of the chin.

Pedro beamed, and said, "You know, Daniel, I saw that Buffalo Bill show and was impressed by the Indians who performed for the crowds..." Glancing appraisingly at Long Knife, he continued. "Is your freend here good with a bow and arrow?"

Seeing a perplexed frown cross Knife's face, Pedro stuttered, "Meaning all respect, Daniel, but please tell your friend to not be offended. It's just that, we are offering heem a job with the show if he wants one. It would make the show complete, sí"

Daniel grinned and glanced at his Indian cousin. "Did you get that, Knife?" he asked.

Knife lifted his nose and tried to act like he wasn't terribly tempted. But, of course, he was. He had watched as his whole village was ground down to a shadow of its former glory. He had held children in his arms as they died of starvation and wept as the old ones in their village crept away in the night to die alone under the stars of their forefathers, rather than take food out of the mouths of babes.

Even now, the people left in his band were weak and hungry and Knife's insides twisted with longing as the fragrance from the gypsy's cook pots filled his nostrils. He had tried to be a good chief to his people, but he knew he had failed. Still, maybe now he could be of some use...

Drawing himself up as tall as possible, he stared Dan in the eyes and asked, "These... travelers would pay me?"

Dan nodded, "Sure, they pay out a percentage of the purse, and all the food you need." Turning to Pedro, he asked, "Ain't that right, Mr. Amaya?"

Pedro knew he had a fish on the line, but also understood that this particular fish had very sharp teeth... and a lot of pride. He asked, "How many people does he have with him? Maybe, we work it out so hees people bring in the meat we need for our cook pots and everyone eats well, but only the men and women who contribute to the show get paid, eh? Does that seem fair, Daniel?"

Knife understood much of what Pedro said, but turned to Dan as if he didn't and whispered, "I think that is a good bargain, Daniel. But can I trust these people?"

Dan shrugged and replied, "I think so, Knife. They saved me from Giddings and have played fair with me since then. Just dress up nice, do some fine bow shooting like you do, and you and your people can travel with us."

Long Knife turned to Pedro and extended his arm. "Me and two of my braves will be your show's Fighting Injuns."

Chapter Forty

THERE ARE THREE ORGANIZATIONS THAT CAN MOBILIZE quickly; the Army, the Indians, and the Gypsies. The next morning proved that fact. By first light, Long Knife's tribe was standing about thirty yards away from the gypsy encampment with all their gear packed up and ready to travel, eating cold biscuits and what remained of yesterday's stew as the Rom finished loading their wagons.

Within an hours' time, the whole procession was on the move. Only the earliest risers on the outskirts of Kuna, saw their passing and wondered when the gypsies would return. Their show had proved a resounding success and many of those left behind felt the loss, as if all the color in the world was fading to black.

It was only a fifteen-mile trip to Nampa, so the procession moved at a leisurely pace, trading jokes, sipping cheap homemade wine, and watching as their new Indian friends rode out occasionally to chase down and kill meat for the cook pots.

Dom Domingo, who often walked while the caravan moved because of his chronic Sciatica moved over to Pedro's wagon. Pedro pulled the horses to a stop and jumped down to hear the Dom's words. "Look at how those Cheyenne hunt, Pedro!" he shook his head. "I have always stuck to the old ways, but I see now that I should have trained the youngsters to hunt, rather than relying on the charity of the gadje, or the skill of our pick-pockets."

Pedro silently agreed, but shook his head and replied, "No, we must adhere to our traditions, Dom. We have wandered all over the world, and I think it would be easy to forget who and what we are. That is what you have done, Dom, upheld our traditions, and I am proud of your work. Still..." he glanced up at the Romany leader with a mischievous grin. "I think that it wouldn't hurt for our young men to learn how to hunt from our new Indian friends, eh?"

Domingo smiled, lifted his left hand in farewell, and strode ahead, his ever-present walking stick clutched in his right hand. Pedro took the opportunity to stretch his legs for a few minutes and let his horses drink from a pail of water since the land they traveled was dry and sere.

Looking about, he saw his son Manny and the youngster, Daniel, arguing about something, almost to the point of shouting. He watched as Manny said something to Daniel and saw the white boy shake his head with a frown. Heart sinking, Pedro hoped that the two young men were not at odds. That would make the success of the show much harder and might lead to the Indian's leaving before they even started!

Daniel suddenly wheeled his horse around and trotted back to where Long Knife's band followed. Pedro looked at his son's face and saw Manny shake his head and dig his heels into his mount's flanks. Trotting up, Manny looked into his father's eyes and said, "Papá, we should talk."

Pedro asked his wife to drive the wagon and he unhitched his gelding that was tied on the back. Mounting up, he waved at Manny to join him and they rode ahead of the caravan to speak privately. Pulling the reins to a slow walk, Pedro turned to his son and said, "Are you and the *gadje* arguing, Manny?"

Manny frowned. "I wish you would not call him so, Papá. He seems to be more like us, or even the Indian people than a "White gadje…"

Pedro nodded, "Yes, you're right and I apologize. You know, the term 'gadje' refers to all people who are not Romany, but I realize the term has taken on the tone of scorn and insult. I did not mean it that way— not to young Daniel."

Manny shrugged. "Yes, Papá, I know," he said, and then fell silent.

Looking at his son's profile, Pedro asked, "So, what is wrong between you two? Will you tell me?"

Manny turned to him and replied, "Yes, of course, Papá. Daniel, he thinks we are all in very grave danger.

His friend, Long Knife, told him that a very bad man named Heck Giddings was behind Daniel's abduction in Laramie. That the banker who held him prisoner at the bank was acting on Gidding's orders."

Pedro shrugged. "Si... so? We escaped from that place with none the wiser. Why does he worry now?"

Manny said, "Papá, Daniel thinks this same man was his father's mortal enemy. He thinks that Giddings wants to kill him... he said that Jake told him to run from that man after he died—that Giddings thinks he is a witness to some old crime."

Pedro rolled his eyes. He truly thought that Daniel was over-dramatizing the situation, but then he recalled something that Dan had read to him and his family after returning from a small outpost with supplies about three weeks earlier.

Pedro liked hearing about the towns his caravan planned to visit. More than once, he had heard news of an outbreak of disease in the next town on their circuit and instructed the caravan to veer away from it, and a couple of times he'd learned that their next stop was filled with people who hated the Rom and were not afraid to chase the gypsies off at the point of a gun.

What tickled his memory now was the name Heck Giddings... wasn't that the name of the man who was running a corrupt campaign of influence and blackmail to have his name at the top of the list for the President to appoint him Wyoming's territorial governor? He shook his head and turned in his saddle to gaze at Daniel and his Indian cousin, Long Knife. On the one hand, Pedro wished the Indian would have kept his mouth shut—he was about to ruin Pedro's plans of monetary solvency for his people. On the other hand, Daniel could be right!

A bad man with power could set many soldiers on his people. Alone, the man would probably not prevail. After all, this caravan had a fine shootist, who was currently training the younger Romany men in the craft. The gypsies, one and all, possessed great skill in knife-work, and now they even had a small band of Cheyenne riding with them. Pedro had seen enough of their bow-work to feel confident they could defend themselves.

He shook his head, and thought, *they would prevail against one man, maybe, si. But a state governor could command whole troops of men! How would his gypsies fare against an army of men intent on putting an end to their young gadje friend?* Turning to face Manny again, Pedro sighed and asked, "So, what does Daniel want to do?"

Manny said, "He thinks he should leave, Papá. I told him he shouldn't think that way—that he worked for us now and was under our protection!" He frowned and added, "Bah! He just said that we-the Rom—are not strong enough to go against a man like Giddings! That made me mad, Papá, and I yelled at him, and he rode away!"

Manny looked so dejected, his father wanted to say, 'Sí, you are right—we will always welcome him and protect him.'

However, every instinct in Pedro's heart told him

that his first concern must be with the Rom and not a gadje outsider. He placed his hand on Manny's shoulders and said, "I must go and talk with Dom Domingo, mi hijo. Please understand that our leader must know of these new developments…"

Manny glared. "What new developments, Father? That Daniel worries about others more than himself? That he worries about everything, all the time? That is hardly new."

Pedro glared right back at his son. "Do you not remember what Daniel read to us a few weeks ago? Unless there are two Heck Giddings, and I doubt that, Daniel's enemy is trying to cheat his way into a presidential appointment as territorial governor of Wyoming! He could bring an army down on us! Now, I like Daniel, truly, I do. But if I do not warn Dom Domingo about what could happen, we might all die for your young gadje friend! Is that what you want?"

Shocked, Manny shook his head, and watched as a train, maybe a half mile away, chugged slowly down a track heading towards the town of Boise.

Chapter Forty-One

THOMAS BLACK AND THREE OTHER MEN FROM HECK Gidding's outfit stepped off the train in Kuna, Idaho. They were all hot, tired and liberally coated with coal dust. They were also frustrated and angry.

The train had been re-routed to accommodate a coal-chute breakdown about 50-miles back, which added an additional seven hours to an already lengthy trip from Laramie. Then, to top off an already trying setback, they learned that the gypsies had up and left the day before.

When asked, Ernest Hickey, the ticket-seller at the depot was eager to share what he knew. "I heard they are heading into Nampa, and then northwest into Oregon and Washington. That's their usual circuit, I guess, although they apparently had a few setbacks this summer. Also, did ya hear? They got them a gunslinger now, and a band of renegade Cheyenne for spice. It's a regular Wild West Show!'

Ernie, a tiny, wizened oldster with no teeth was obviously a fan of the gypsy show and seemed totally unaware of his audience's hostile response to his words. He would have continued speaking but Tom, weary of the man's worshipful tone barked, "We ain't askin' if you like those Gyps, but where they are now. Also, is that young gunslinger still ridin' with them?"

Ernie abruptly stopped talking and gazed up at the four heavily armed and tough-looking men who were staring down at him with anger. A chill ran down his spine as he realized that he'd let his mouth run away with his good sense, yet again, and stammered, "Oh yeah. Sorry, Fellers, I thought I'd already said—they're heading to Nampa right now. That's about fifteen miles west of here. And... yeah, the kid is a new part of their show, I guess."

Tom asked, "When is the next train?"

"The next train won't come through until tomorrow," Ernie said. "But ten dollars will rent ya a coach if'n you want one. Of course, you could always ride... ain't but two days, unless you wanted to put on a bunch of speed, but then you might ruin your mount. Pretty tough going out there and no water-holes..."

Ernie would have kept on going, but suddenly all four men turned on their heels and crowded out the front door of the train depot. Staring after them, Ernie scratched his head and wondered what to do. It seemed plain as day to him that those men carried ill intentions toward the Gypsies, and Ernie couldn't understand it.

Why? He wondered, uneasily. He had grown fond of

the Romany people over the past few years; well, ever since his Matilda passed away in 1879. There was a certain old Granny traveling with the band who made it possible for him to communicate with his wife of forty-seven years. He missed her so, but now, he also missed that certain old granny whose name was Nanette...

Ernie's eyes grew bright as he recalled Nanette's soft brown eyes, her lilting voice and her old, wrinkled hands that were also as soft as velvet. Then he blushed. He was as infatuated as a pup and embarrassed by his crush. Still, those men had murder in their eyes and he did not want Nanette or her people to come to any harm.

Turning around, he marched into the back office and smiled at the shiny new telegraph machine that had been delivered and installed earlier that spring. Technically, the operator was not supposed to send private messages on the machine, but Ernie knew that meant *everyone*, even the operator, was supposed to pay for the privilege.

So, he pulled a leather coin purse from his trouser pocket and put two bits for a telegram into the service-pay envelope. Then he sat and typed a telegram to the Nampa Hotel; where his good friend, Marty Drummond, who also loved the gypsies, worked the front desk and telegraph machine.

He warned Monty that four bad players were headed into town and he thought they were after the gypsies, and maybe even the young white man who rode with them. He asked his old friend to warn Dom Domingo about the threat and then told Monty to take care of himself while he was at it. He signed it—**Your friend, Ernest Hickey**— and then sat back with a satisfied expression on his face.

He was no one special, he knew, but he could spot a gunslinger from a mile away, and he remembered a saying that went something like—"the pen is mightier than the sword."

Nodding, he thought, *those men think they're powerful with their big guns and bad attitudes, but I got the drop on them, didn't I?*

———

A COUPLE of hours after he rode away from his friend Manny, Daniel rode up and said, "Howdy…"

Manny looked over and said, "Hola, Daniel. Are you feeling better now?"

Dan nodded. "Yeah. Hey, sorry about getting all huffy. I didn't mean to… I just get so antsy sometimes, I don't know what to do to make things right."

Manny shrugged. "It's okay, Daniel. I understand. Listen, I talked to Papá about it and he agrees with you."

Dan looked surprised and suddenly uneasy. "You mean, he thinks I should go, too?"

Manny shook his head. "I don't know what has been decided, Daniel. He is meeting with Dom Domingo now. He should be back pretty soon, though."

Dan laughed. "It's kinda funny, because Long Knife just told me that there's safety in numbers and I shouldn't take off on my own. I came to tell you that I had changed my mind about leaving!"

Manny frowned. "Daniel, *mi* Papá does not want you to leave. He cares for you and he likes what you and your gun are doing for our success. It's just that he felt the Dom should know about what's going on. Tell me you understand, eh? I would feel terrible about losing your friendship because of my big mouth!"

Dan shrugged. "No, it's for the best. Whether I stay or go, the gypsies need to know what's going on. If I stay they will be prepared and if I go, they won't have to worry about me, right?"

Relieved, Manny nodded. "Sí, Daniel. Ride with me, okay? We will not have to wait long to find out what the Dom decides."

Chapter Forty-Two

TWENTY MINUTES LATER PEDRO RODE UP TO WHERE HIS son and Daniel walked their horses at a slow pace. He smiled and waved one hand. "Come you two, let's ride ahead so we can talk in private."

Pedro turned his horse about and suddenly feeling a wild sense of abandon, kicked the gelding's flanks hard. The sturdy old horse pricked his ears and leapt ahead. Manny grinned, not having seen his Papá do this sort of thing for many years, although Pedro had once been one of the Rom's best and fastest riders.

The three riders flew past the slow-moving caravan, much to the delight of the gypsies who hooted and hollered as Pedro and Manny pulled their feet from the stirrups and climbed atop their saddles to stand and give their compatriots a smile and a bow. For extra spice, Manny bent down, grabbed ahold of the saddle and performed a galloping hand-stand.

Dan, who was a barely adequate rider, shook his

head and grinned. These people continually amazed him. On one hand; they were humble, shy and religious, and on the other, unabashed thieves and tricksters who thought nothing of robbing a 'mark' blind. Their unbelievable skill with horses and knives was nothing to remark upon—to them it was nothing more than heritage that must be kept alive.

The three raced about a mile ahead of the caravan and finally pulled to a stop. Pedro and his son were laughing so hard they could barely cling to their saddles, and Dan accused, "You two scared the life outta me, you know!"

The gypsies burst out laughing again, and Manny said, "Don't worry, Daniel. We will teach you how to ride…" He glanced at his father and grew serious, "Won't we, Papá?"

Pedro grinned. "Sí, Manny." Turning to Dan he added, "I told the Dom about your problems with that gadje outlaw, and about how you were worried about the Rom. He says for you to stand by us, and so we will stand by you. Besides, maybe you worry over nothing? I remember that this enemy of your father might become the governor of Wyoming? Maybe he is too busy with the election campaign to worry about the son of a dead foe."

Dan nodded. He was thankful he didn't have to leave—just yet. He realized that his new allies were just as tough in their own way as Giddings and his men. Still, the tone of voice Jake had used on his deathbed… the dread and fear that was so unlike the man he knew and had grown to love was too real to be ignored.

Smiling, he extended his right hand and said, "Thank you so much, Mr. Amaya. I will do my best to make you proud. Just... just keep your eyes peeled, okay? He has a lot of men, I hear, to do his dirty-work for him."

Pedro had moved forward to shake Daniel's hand when his eyes grew wide. Dan saw panic in the man's face and saw Manny's mouth drop at the same moment Pedro's horse snorted and reared backward. In fact, all the horses were squealing in fright and Dan turned around to see an enormous brown bear charging at them from the tree line about fifty-yards away.

A grizzly!, he thought and seeing two tiny, big-eared bears hiding in the brush watching, he realized that one of the biggest sows he'd ever seen was bearing down on them like a run-away freight train. She had probably watched their rapid approach and judged them a threat to her brood. Even as these thoughts ran through his head, his hands pulled the revolvers on his hips and he started shooting.

One by one, as Pedro and Manny ran away shouting in fear and all the horses scattered, Dan shot his revolvers. Right hand—*Boom!* Left-hand—*Boom!* Over and over, Dan stood his ground and emptied his guns. Still, the giant bear kept coming.

Dan was unaware of the sweat that had popped from his brow and now ran down his face in streaks. Each of his pistols held six bullets and he'd used them all! He knew he was about to die and his heart pounded in his ears like a kettledrum. Then, he dropped his left-hand gun and placed one more bullet in his right-hand pistol. His left hand shook with nerves, but good training and instinct took over. When the bear was less than six-feet away, he aimed for the bear's right eye. *Boom!*

The bear roared and then dropped to the ground in a heap of blood, fur and dust. She skidded so hard and so fast her body rolled right over the top of Dan who collapsed, screaming, under her weight.

Dan passed out then from nerves and pain. Although his last shot had gone clean through the bear's brain, killing it instantly, her tumble twisted Dan's left ankle and landed on his chest so hard he cracked a couple of ribs.

Pedro and Manny approached cautiously and saw that the beast was dead, but Dan lay pale and still under it's body. They mourned the brave boy's loss until he opened one blue eye and murmured, "You gonna stand there all day, or are you gonna help me out?"

Chapter Forty-Three

SEEING THREE LATHERED AND RIDER-LESS HORSES galloping back to the caravan alerted the gypsies that something had happened to Pedro and the two boys. Dom Domingo stepped up on the closest wagon and hollered, "We must hurry, something has happened to our friends! Be careful, though, we may have to fight."

The gypsies laid to with their reins, urging their wagons and horses ahead with speed but Long Knife and three of his braves rode past the caravan whooping and screaming in defiance of an unseen enemy. As they crested a low rise, Knife saw that Daniel and the two gypsies were limping slowly back toward the caravan. Pedro and Manny held Daniel between them, though, and even from a distance Knife could see his young friend's face was twisted with pain.

Then, looking past them, he saw a large pile of dark fur and squinting, saw that a very large bear lay in a heap on the ground. He dug his heels in his horse's flanks and rode toward his young friend.

Even as he rode up, he saw Daniel smile and heard Pedro cry out, "Long Knife! See those bear cubs? *Por favor*, try to grab them for us. They would make a fine addition to our show!"

Knife glanced to where Pedro was pointing and saw two baby bears by the tree line barking and bawling in fear. He rolled his eyes. *A waste of good meat*, he thought, but he signaled to his men to go and fetch the cubs, alive, if possible. Meanwhile, he studied Daniel's face and saw that his eyes were wide with pride and excitement even though his cheeks were pale with some unseen injury.

Knife slid off his horse's back and walked up to his cousin. "Daniel, what happened? Are you injured?"

Dan grinned. "That bear back yonder charged us, but I managed to put it down before it could get to us. She rolled over me, though, and I think my ankle is banged up." He shrugged, wincing. "Also," he added, "it hurts to breathe… might have busted a couple of ribs." He eyes shone and he said, "I did some pretty good shootin' though, Knife. Jake would have been proud, I think."

Manny nodded, "Si, Daniel saved our lives, Long Knife. He is a hero!"

Knife gazed at the young man his uncle Jake had adopted and knew that Jake was, even now, smiling at his protégé's skill and bravery. Still, being Indian and not prone to public displays of praise, he snorted and said, "That's what you get for closing your eyes to what is around you when you ride. You were all showing off when you rode ahead of the rest of us and paying no attention to your surroundings. You could have gotten yourselves killed!"

His words brought the men back down to earth—especially Pedro, who had already realized that his hijinks were careless, if not downright dangerous. Seeing the caravan quickly approaching, he sighed, knowing that he would probably hear the same lecture from Dom Domingo as soon as he heard about what happened.

Knife and the others turned when they heard panicked grunts and squeals coming from a couple of cloth bags the Indian's had draped over their horses' necks. Both braves grinned in triumph, although one of them complained loudly about a deep scratch on his right arm. Apparently, one of the cubs had fought back before being bagged.

Then, the caravan was upon them and Dan was swooped off to abuela Nanette's wagon for doctoring, the cubs were introduced to a man named Sergei Katovich who had once trained with the Russian Circus, and the Indians were busily skinning and quartering the dead grizzly.

A LITTLE WHILE LATER, Dan sat on Granny's bed and stared at Manny's big sister with longing. Maria was wrapping cloth bindings around his ribs with soft but firm fingers while Nanette was concocting a foul-smelling poultice for his sprained ankle. Both women were chattering like magpies and shooting amused looks in his direction. He had the distinct impression they were making fun of him and he felt mortified.

Dan realized, suddenly, that he was always trying to make a good impression when Maria was near, and he understood now that he was a fool. He would always be a laughingstock to her—just a little boy with his toy gun. If his feelings weren't so hurt, he would be hopping mad!

Pride in his accomplishment fell away and he abruptly felt the pain of his injuries. His left ankle had swollen to twice its normal size and throbbed wretchedly, and his cracked ribs burned with every breath he took. Looking away, he tried to hide his misery from the two woman who thought he was so funny.

Then, Nanette sat down on the edge of the bed and gently took ahold of his left foot. He gasped, and she hissed at him when he tried to pull away. Then, she smiled sweetly, and placed the brown and green potion on his ankle. He groaned as the cold brew touched his skin and then, like a miracle, the pain eased.

Maria wrapped the ankle in more soft bindings and then she moved up the side of the bed and leaned over to stare into Daniel's face. He felt almost too shy to meet her gaze, but he finally looked up.

To his complete shock and amazement, she bent down and placed her ripe, red lips on his. Even as he reveled in his first kiss, she pulled away slightly, and whispered, "Bravo, Daniel. Bravo!"

Then, she was gone, and he was left only with the secret, smiling eyes of abuela Nanette.

Chapter Forty-Four

THE HONORABLE JUDGE DAVID KOATS PACED BACK AND forth between his desk and the sitting area where his father and son sat waiting for him to sit down and talk reasonably about the situation they were in.

Politics was and had always been a risky venture—here in the new territory of Wyoming, and back home in South Carolina. David knew this and had gone into the governor's race with his eyes wide open—or so he thought. He knew when he and his family had moved here that they were moving into a Republican enclave, and an area where most of the citizens had favored the Northern aggressors in the Civil War.

But that situation was fluid. The Koat's family had been here since 1872 and in that time, the population had ebbed and flowed—sometimes bringing great crowds of Southern sympathizers and sometimes over-flowing with Northern pilgrims, intent on colonizing the new western states. Things had changed, however, when the Republican candidate, Chester A. Arthur, was voted in as president of the United States.

Now, even die-hard democrats were defecting to the right and David could feel his grasp on the governor's race weakening every day. That was alright, though. He still had a job as a circuit judge for Wyoming and Southern Idaho, and he knew that unfortunate timing was often the reason a political campaign failed.

What he couldn't tolerate was the man the people in this territory were voting into office. Were they blind? Couldn't they see what Heck Giddings was? He sat down on the divan and glared at his father. "Are the people in this state really that blind? Can't they see that Giddings is nothing more than a thug?"

Adam Koats shrugged. "Gidding's has deep pockets, son. The support coming his way is either being bought or exhorted from voters who don't care which party controls the territorial governor's house—just so they can control it."

David threw back his head and laughed. "Gidding's is no more a Republican or Democrat than I am! Honestly, I don't think he has a political bone in his body. The two or three times we've met, he hasn't been able to answer one single question about how he plans to run the territory. Whenever I ask his opinion on anything political, he clams up and turns to his mouthpiece—a man by the name of Percy McIver. It's unnerving, really, like a man with a mannequin.

David's son, Oliver, spoke up. "Can our finances survive the loss, father?"

David couldn't help but glare. He had, indeed, spent a fortune in the political race for governor, but the Koat's fortune was deep, and steadfast. Oliver spent far too much time and energy worrying about his inheritance than was seemly, and always raised questions if he felt his mother or father were spending any of what he considered *his* personal fortune.

"Don't you worry about that, Olly. Listen, don't you have a horse race to attend? I can't make it, but I told my friends that you would be there..."

Blushing, Oliver knew he was being dismissed. He loved his mamma and papa, really, he did. But they both seemed to treat the family fortune with reckless abandon, and he had no intention of spending his maturity in poverty.

He had expansive tastes, after all; a string of gorgeous racing horses, a large and beautiful estate to maintain, and a spoiled, high-end wife to support. How could he maintain his lifestyle if his father lost all his stake in a country bumpkin governor's race?

Knowing that his own greed had reared its ugly head, though, and that both his father and his grandfather had glimpsed the extent of it and were not pleased, he smiled, placed his fancy new bowler on his head and gave a slight bow. "You're right as rain, Dad, as usual. I'm sorry for my careless words—you know best how to handle our family's assets. I'll be off now. Have a good day, Grandfather!"

He turned and left the room while David and Adam watched. Once he was gone, David sighed. "That boy... what will it take to make him happy, I wonder? He was already given a fortune when he turned twenty-five, but now it seems that he's broke again and just counting down the minutes until I die."

Adam glared. "He's been spoiled, David, and you know it! I blame Emily, who never let her son's hands get dirty."

David held his own mitts in the air. "Please, father, let's not quarrel about my wife! I know she hasn't been the best influence on Olly's upbringing, but she married down when she married me. She could have married *anyone,* but she settled for a farmer's son, and I owe her for that!"

Adam glowered but remained silent. *Sure,* he thought, *I was a plantation owner, that's all. But I was a good one and amassed a fortune. And my son worked hard at farming as well as in college. He is a fine and well-respected lawyer and judge and he needn't bow his head to anyone! Especially a cotton-headed ninny like Emily!*

Emily had always put on airs and the passage of time had not softened her hard edges, but he loved David and wanted his only son to be happy. Deciding not to foul the air any further with talk about Emily and her rotten-egg offspring, he said, "You're right, son, and I'm sorry. Let's talk a little more about what we can do to salvage this election. Heck Giddings isn't territorial governor yet. With a little work on our part, he might never claim that honor."

———

OLIVER DROVE his fancy black buggy to the far end of town and stopped in front of a saloon called the Rumpled Skirt Café. The rather risqué title had originated respectfully enough in the early 1870's because the building had once been a restaurant on the main stage line, and many a lady had arrived in town with her skirts in a bunch from the long stage ride coming from and going to Laramie.

The old, dilapidated building had changed hands more than once, however, since then and now housed one of the seedier brothels in town. Honestly, Oliver didn't like even soiling the seat of his britches by sitting down in the place, but this is where Mr. Giddings wanted to meet, and if Oliver was to get his (father's) money back in the upcoming election, he had better follow orders.

He stepped inside and saw Giddings sitting at his usual table toward the back of the room. He was approached more than once by prostitutes that reeked of sweat and unwashed small-clothes and shook his head at their offers. "No! Thank you, but no," he mumbled as the women draped their arms over his starchy black suit.

He tried to hide his dismay. *I'll need to have my suit coat laundered before I go home, or Sophia will wonder where I've been!* His disgust was so transparent, Giddings couldn't help but smirk.

Oliver Koats was such a pantywaist, it was no

wonder his dear old dad was losing the election. *Sure,* Giddings thought, *I'm greasing a few palms in my bid for governor, but what politician doesn't!*

Still, what was really turning the tide in Gidding's direction was Oliver's efforts to undermine his father's influence amongst the cities elite. Offering the kid a hundred dollars for every vote that swung his way had been a stroke of genius on Heck's part, and he couldn't help but feel a little sorry for his opponent, Judge David Koats.

What knife cuts deeper than a son's betrayal?, he wondered as the young man sat down at his table, remembering Jake and how his betrayal still cut him to his very core.

Chapter Forty-Five

TOM BLACK AND HIS THREE COMRADES, HARRY BATRE, Clarence White and Steve Powell, arrived in the town of Nampa and stared about in dismay. Like Kuna, this town was a one street railroad town with only a few houses, one church, a hotel, two saloons, a post office/mercantile, a blacksmith's shack, a solicitor's office, a sheriff's office/jail, and one café.

The four men could clearly see from one end of town to the other and beyond. They saw no sign of a gypsy caravan and they looked to one another with confusion. They were also quite tired, as they'd ridden their horses hard to find their quarry.

The question now was: Had the gypsies already come and gone, or were they late? Instead of pondering the situation, Tom said, "Let's go and have a drink, boys. We'll find out where those Gyps are while we wet our whistles."

The sun was setting over a series of tall buttes to the

west of town and casting red and gold bars of molten light onto the street as the gunslingers made their way to the closest bar. It was a Friday night and they could hear tinkling glassware and raucous laughter from the front stoop.

There were a few broadsheets pinned by the front door and Black paused to study a flyer that read:

Come one, Come all
To Dom Domingo's Circus
Extravaganza!
Featuring:
Exotic Food and Drink,
Knife Work,
Horse Racing,
Fortune Telling,
And the World's youngest Gunslinger,
Daniel the Two-Shooter!
August 15-21st!

Black snorted. *Daniel the two-shooter? The four of us will see about that,* he thought. Then he remembered today's date. It was now the 22nd of August. *Where are those damn Gyps?,* he wondered. Pushing the bat-wing doors open he stepped inside the bar, followed by Gidding's other hired guns.

Looking about, Black spied an empty table by the back wall and led the way to sit down for a few drinks. They were met by a waitress who hurried ahead of them to wipe the dirty table down. She was just seventeen, the barkeep's daughter; and as she bent over to scrub the table, Black stood behind her, placed his hands on both her hips and made a couple of thrusting motions. His companions roared with laughter, the girl blushed as red as a tomato and many of the men in the bar stopped talking and glared over at them in anger.

Young Millicent was a sweet kid and loved by many of the town's citizens. If her ma hadn't of died from scarlet fever, little Millie wouldn't have even been allowed inside the saloon, but since Alice was deceased, along with her stillborn son, Milly had been forced to help her pa out waiting tables.

Up until now, thanks to the local citizens, the girl had not been molested, but this rough-looking man had just laid hands on and most of the men watching wanted to teach him and his friends a lesson. Still— their eyes dropped, and their hands stilled as they took their measure of the four strangers in their midst.

Chances are, I'll end up in a shallow grave if I pull a gun on one of those bad hombres, many of them thought, correctly. After a moment or two of tense silence the customers started talking again, and Millie fled out the back door as the four strangers stared about in defiance.

The bar's owner, Thaddeus Adams, walked to the table with a basket of peanuts and asked, "What can I bring you gents?" His cheeks were mottled pink and red with impotent rage but knew better than to incur the men's wrath by refusing service.

He'd sent Millie home for the night, and

temporarily hired her beau, Stephen Fairbanks, to help him work the bar. Both Thaddeus and Stephen had seen the big, scar-faced man shame Millicent, and both wanted to put their fists through the man's face. But Thaddeus, Millie's father, needed to stay alive to protect his only child, and Stephen was a consumptive and couldn't hit the backside of a barn with two bullets, his eyesight was so poor.

Black grinned and answered, "Four glasses and a bottle of your best whiskey. Do you serve supper?"

Thaddeus shook his head, "No sir. But the café stays open until 9:00. They serve a good stew and have the best pies in the county."

"Okay, fine. Now, hurry up with that bottle," Black said and sat back in his seat.

A few moments later a bottle and four glasses appeared at their table, and the men set-to quenching their thirst. Finally, Black set his glass down and asked in a loud voice, "Anybody in here know where those Gyps are? Poster out front said they should be here by now."

One fellow, who had come late to the party and missed what the man had done to little Millie said, "They're back a ways—set up in the woods due to some sort of accident, is what I heard. They're coming in next Tuesday, though."

"That right..." Black said, "What kinda accident, do you know?"

The old man shrugged, uncomfortably aware suddenly, of his peers' disapproval of his continuing discussion with the four strangers. Deciding to end his part in the transaction, he mumbled, "Don't rightly know." Then he took a long draw off his beer mug and looked away.

Black felt rage rise in his chest. Maybe it was because he knew the old man was holding back, or maybe he knew that the men in this bar had suddenly seen him and his companions for what they were— apex predators on the hunt. Like a flock of sheep, they sensed the presence of wolves and were now huddling together for comfort and support.

Lately, whenever this sort of thing happened, Tom felt a queasy mix of shame and pride—he had not started out life with the intention of being a bad man— in fact, he had once striven to do the right thing and walk with God as much as possible. But circumstances changed a man and the things Heck Giddings had demanded of him over the long decades had changed Black into an evildoer.

Sometimes, like tonight, his shame got the better of him and when that happened, he not only saw red, but bathed in it. He stood up as the saloon grew as silent as a graveyard and turned around to face old Wiley Burroughs. He slowly drew his pistol out of it's holster, aimed it at Burroughs forehead and said, "You better tell me where those Gyps are, and the kid that's riding with them or you'll be facing your maker in about five seconds flat. Hear me?"

Burroughs started trembling violently, and a couple of his friends saw a thin yellow stream of urine drip from his chair and over-flow onto the sawdust-covered floor boards. He held his hands up in the air, and squeaked, "Honestly, I'm not sure exactly where they're at but I heard they're about five miles back toward Kuna, pulled into the woods on the south side of the main road. Please, buddy, don't shoot me!"

"What was this accident you talked about?" Black hissed.

"A bear was what I heard—that young shooter they got with them put the creature down, but he was injured. Please, mister, that's all I know, I swear it!"

As quickly as the rage came, it disappeared and Black grinned. Holstering his pistol, he turned around, picked up the quickly diminishing whiskey bottle, and took a long pull.

So, Black thought, *our quarry is injured, and the gypsies are all alone out in the woods, away from public scrutiny. Plus, they are days away from even showing up in Nampa. This is getting better and better. Now, we can rest our horses, grab a bite to eat and stay in the town's hotel for the night. Then, in the morning we can ride out and shoot the whole lot of them—none the wiser.*

Suddenly, feeling his appetite roar to life, Tom Black drank the last of the whiskey and said, "Let's go boys. I'm starving."

Clarence asked, "We ain't going after them now?"

Tom frowned. "Nah, our horses need to cool down and we could all use a little rest. Those gyps ain't going nowhere."

Clarence nodded, and the four men stood up and

walked past the old gentleman with jeers of scorn as Burroughs sat huddled in a pool of his own pee, tears of shame running down his cheeks. Every man in the bar felt shaken and Thaddeus hurried over to his friend with a large towel and an overcoat to hide his shame.

Another man crept to the window and peered through the burlap curtains at the four gunslingers as they crossed the street and stepped inside Maddy's Café. Marty Drummond had received a cryptic message from his old buddy, Ernie, three days earlier and instantly knew that these men were the bad characters who seemed intent on hurting Dom Domingo's gypsies and even the young shooter who rode with them.

He stepped back to the bar, quickly downed his nightly brandy, patted Burroughs on the back and headed outside. Mounting up, he headed east for a speedy, moonlit ride.

Chapter Forty-Six

FIVE MILES TO THE EAST, JUAN SAT ON A LOG STARING out over the moonlit prairie. He was stationed about two-hundred yards away from the gypsy encampment. It was his turn to do guard duty, along with three other men—all of them facing toward the four points of the compass. The moon was so big and bright he could see the trees, shrubs and groundswells laid out before his eyes in stark relief.

It was easy duty—a lot easier than staring through the darkness to try and spot incoming threats. Still, despite the luminous beauty of the warm summer night, Juan's heart was dark with shadows of anger and resentment.

Lately, no matter what he tried to do to prove his worth as a man, that white gadje niño took all the attention—and praise—away from Juan, and he was sick of it! Sure, he may have done a few things in the past that made his people angry, but that was in his reckless youth. He was a man now! More importantly, he was Rom, and Daniel was nothing but a stupid white boy—not even worthy of the Rom's scorn.

Still, he was bringing fresh cash to the gypsies, and showed steady nerve when faced with that charging bear. Now, even Maria Amaya seemed taken in with the boy's blue eyes and winsome smile. Juan gritted his teeth in anger. Maria was not his, and never would be —she was promised to his good friend Rafé, but it was entirely improper for Rafe's intended to make eyes at another man—especially a white man!

Juan started to scheme, completely unaware that this kind of behavior was precisely why his fellow Rom mistrusted him and his self-serving ways. He had just decided to sow seeds of doubt about Maria in Rafé's ears the following morning when he heard rapidly approaching hoofbeats coming up the road from the town of Nampa.

Heart pounding with nervous tension, he stood up and peered down the road, seeing a solitary horse and rider heading their way. Juan fingered the hilt of his knife, wishing all over again that Dom Domingo would trust him with one of the gypsies few guns. *Just another thing to be angry about...* he thought.

As the rider drew near, however, Juan relaxed. It was only that old white man—what was his name, again? Drummer? No, Drummond, si, Marty Drummond from Nampa. Juan stepped away from the log and held a hand up in the air, as the old man drew his horse to a stop. "*¡Alto!* What is your business here at this time of night?' he demanded in a nasty tone of voice.

Marty's eyes grew wide. He hadn't risked life and limb, nor the safety of his horse by riding in the dark to be rudely interrogated by one of the gypsies he was trying to save! He cleared his throat, and said, "Listen, I need to talk to Dom Domingo... we're friends. I have news he needs to hear right away."

Juan shook his head and sneered. All the prejudice and hatred he'd ever felt about the gadjes and their world suddenly roared to life in his breast and he took the opportunity to let those feelings loose. "Friends! You are no friend to the Rom—especially not to our leader, Dom Domingo! He hates all you stupid gadje! Now, turn your horse around and go back home! We do not want you here! ¡*Andele*! Go, now!"

Marty's shoulders drooped, and his old heart felt pierced to the quick. He had always admired the gypsies and had been one of their most ardent advertisers, but now he knew they had only barely tolerated him. He felt his words of warning turn to ashes on his tongue and he turned his horse around to head home.

Juan grinned as Marty rode away, looking like a kicked dog. Then, the oldster's shoulders straightened, and he stopped his horse. Turning around in his saddle, Marty drew in a deep breath and hollered, "You may not like me and my kind over-much, but I came out here to tell you that there are four pistol packers headed this way!"

Marty stared at Juan who was visibly flinching at

the man's shouts. Then he continued, "Boy! Daniel the Two-Shooter, or whatever your name is, I think they're after you, too! Better be ready, okay? I'm going home now," he finished, faced forward again and walked his horse back to the road, as Juan cursed in frustration.

———

ABOUT A HALF HOUR EARLIER, Dan had rolled over in his sleep and gasped out loud in agony. Grandma Nanette had given him a powerful tea earlier that evening to help dull the discomfort, but the effects had apparently worn off, and now his pain rang like a bell and he was wide awake with beads of sweat standing out on his forehead.

Worse, he had to pee, and he knew if he didn't get up soon, he would wet Nanette's cozy bed. Sighing, he drew his feet over the side of the tick mattress and gingerly placed his right foot on the wagon's floor-boards. He grabbed a gnarled walking stick by the side of the mattress, then gently placed his swollen ankle on the floor.

There was a bright flash of pain, but Dan took two deep breaths and stood up. He wobbled in place for a moment but knowing there was nothing to do but go forward, he made his way outside trying to keep his grunts of discomfort as quiet as could be.

Nanette and her granddaughter Maria were sleeping together in a small tent to the side of the wagon and Dan moved away so as not to disturb their slumber. He hobbled slowly toward the privy ditch that had been dug to the west of the encampment and after a few minutes, he was leaning one hand on a tree and sighing with relief as he emptied his bladder.

He was just shaking off and getting ready to make his way back to Nanette's wagon when he heard a man hollering in the distance. He couldn't help but wonder —*is this an attack?* Looking at the moon's position in the sky, he judged the time at about midnight. *Who would be hollering just outside our perimeter but someone either in trouble or asking for it!*

He winced as he made up his mind and moved forward as silently as possible to see what was going on. That's when he heard a man shout, "You may not like me and my kind over-much, but I came out here to tell you that there are four pistol packers headed this way!"

There was a moment of silence and then the man added, "Boy! Daniel the Two-Shooter, or whatever your name is, I think they're after you, too! Better be ready, okay? I'm going home now."

Dan started to shake as the man's words registered in his mind. It was Giddings! He knew it in his gut!

It only took a second to decide, and then Dan moved swiftly toward Pedro Amaya's hut to spread the news. All he knew was, now the gypsies were in as much trouble as he was, and if he didn't warn them quickly, he and all his new friends would die.

Chapter Forty-Seven

TOM BLACK AWOKE THE NEXT MORNING WITH A pounding head, a sore throat and a lurching wave of nausea. "Gah!," he groaned and sat up in the bed with a wince. Feeling something move next to him under the dirty sheets, he looked down and saw the tousled red hair of the prostitute he'd brought up to his room the night before.

He frowned and scratched his head, trying to remember the previous nights' misadventures. He recalled heading into the town's café and having a decent supper—tasty venison stew, biscuits, peaches and a large piece of cherry pie. Then, he and his men had stepped back outside and spied another saloon at the far end of town.

Making their way down the boardwalk, all three men started grinning as they spied a red light flickering behind one of the bar's windows. *Whores! Now, this is more like it!*, they thought. Sure enough, several scantily-dressed women milled about the seedy saloon, sitting on the male customer's laps, serving drinks, and singing around a player-piano in the far, back corner.

Things got a little fuzzy in Tom's mind after that, so he stood up and weaved his way over to the chamber pot. Letting loose a powerful stream, he barked, "Hey you, wake up and skedaddle!"

The woman stirred but simply turned over and made herself comfortable on his pillow. Done emptying his bladder, that red bloom of rage blossomed in Tom's chest again, and he strode over to the bed, grabbed the woman's ratty red hair and hauled her out from under the covers. Startled awake, the girl screeched as she hit the floor with a hard bounce.

"Gawd-dangit!" she howled. "What in the hell is your problem?" she whined as she picked herself up off the floor.

"I told you, leave before I kick your fat ass outta here!" Tom snarled.

The whore, whose name was Prudy said, "All right! All right—jeez!" She hastily pulled her tattered gown over her head, grabbed her boots, gave him a nasty glare and left the room, slamming the door behind her.

He could hear her yelling insults as she made her way downstairs, but he turned away and picked up the whiskey bottle he'd brought in the night before. Gulping a little 'hair of the dog', he sat back down on the side of the bed, nursing his aching head. *God!*, he thought, *what kind of rot-gut was that bar serving us last night? Poison, pure and simple!*

His head was banging him so hard, it felt like a herd of wild ponies were milling around in his brainpan—sounded like it, too. He laid his source of torment back down on the pillow, smelling the girl's cheap perfume, and tried to get back to sleep.

Unfortunately, instead of relaxing, the noises in his head grew louder, and he grunted with displeasure. He pulled the pillow up over his ears and had almost drifted off to sleep again, but then he sat up and grumbled, "What the hell?"

The noise he heard was not in his head, he realized, but coming from the street outside! He stood up and walked over to the window. Looking down from the second floor, his mouth dropped as he saw about ten brightly-colored wagons; maybe twenty-five horses, mules and ponies, several cook fires, three tipis, and a few men and boys setting up a racetrack fifty yards from Main Street.

Their arrival had also awoken the townsfolk who were just now making their way outside to welcome their much-anticipated guests. He saw his former lady-friend, Prudy, chatting up a handsome, dark-haired gypsy man and saw the Gyp's teeth flash brightly in the morning sun. *She sure is friendly with that Gyp, whereas she acted about half disgusted by me...* he thought with resentment.

Tom was awake enough now to realize he'd made a mistake by choosing to stay in town last night and party rather than head out, first thing, for the gypsy's camp. Gritting his teeth, he knew that despite feeling like crap, he needed to get sharp and mobilize his men for action.

Tom Black glared furiously, and then he relaxed. The main thing he and the boys needed to do was get that kid. And their orders clearly said: DEAD or ALIVE. Smiling wolfishly, he decided that things were okay, after all. He only needed to send his boys outside to move in and isolate Dan Monroe, while he hid safe and snug in his hotel room and sniped him to death from above.

———

ABOUT SEVEN HOURS EARLIER, Dan had made his way to Mr. Amayas's wagon and hissed, "Mr. Amaya! Sorry, Pedro wake up, please!"

He heard a grunt from inside the covered wagon and then the canvas door flap opened, and Pedro was blinking out at him. "Sí? Daniel, what is it?" Looking around, he added, "What time is it?"

Dan said, "I'm sorry Mr. Amaya, but it's late—probably about 1:30 in the morning, but you must listen to what I have to say... please!"

Pedro heard panic in the boy's voice and asked, "What is it? Tell me."

It only took a few minutes and then Pedro ran over to the Dom's wagon to tell Domingo the news. An hour later, the camp was on the move. Just before they beat a hasty retreat, Dom Domingo called Juan over to his side.

"Where were you tonight, Juan... facing north, south, east or west?" Domingo asked, gently enough.

Juan looked half ill with nerves, and the moon's light showed the whites of his eyes as he pondered his Dom's question. "I, er... I was facing west, Dom. I think."

"You think, Juan? You think?" Suddenly Dom Domingo was roaring in anger, and Juan was cringing back from his leader in fear. "We heard about what you said to that nice old gadje when he came out here to warn of us danger, and we also know you ignored his warning!"

Juan put his hands in the air, and demanded, "Tell me who accuses me... I will end him!"

Domingo stood silent for a moment and then drew back his right hand and slapped Juan's left cheek. Juan placed his hand on his burning face and stared up at his Dom with sullen eyes. Domingo hissed, "I have always known you as a slacker and a liar, Juan, but this is too much! We are leaving now and going to a public place, so we are not assassinated in our sleep. But, you are not going with us—no!"

Juan's mouth dropped open and he stared around at the disembarking caravan in shock. "What do you men, Dom? This is my home—my people!"

Domingo shook his head. "No, no longer, Juan. You have betrayed us once too many times, and now you have put us in grave peril. I suggest you get on your wagon and ride into the state of Washington. There is another band of Romany there, just outside of the town of Yakima. Maybe they will take you—but you are no longer welcome here."

With those words, Dom Domingo walked away to put together some last-minute plans for when they reached the town of Nampa. He knew that his people would need to dig deep into their own history to pull off their means of escape from the men who pursued them. Shaking his head in disgust, he walked up to Pedro's wagon, called some of his best pickpockets forward and shared his plans for the fair tomorrow, as Juan stood as still as a stone, tears of remorse running from his eyes.

Chapter Forty-Eight

TOM BLACK DRESSED QUICKLY AND STRODE DOWN THE hall to awaken his men. Steve and Clancy were passed-out cold but Harry, a grey-haired, gimlet-eyed veteran, was wide-awake and sober as a church mouse. Harry Batre had a deep and abiding hatred for alcoholic spirits of any kind and only drank milk or coffee.

He answered the door to Tom's knock and waited for his orders. He had seen the caravan roll into town before the sun even rose and had silently cursed his companion's lack of discipline. He had been ready for action for hours but remained silent and respectful when Black told him to go and set eyes on the kid, Dan Monroe.

The other two men were not so easily roused but finally, Clancy and Steve were walking through the gathering crowds with painful, bloodshot eyes and pounding heads. Harry had already reported back to

Tom that if the kid was with the Gyps, at all, he was staying well-hidden.

Tom frowned. "Well, unless something happened, I know he's acting as a sharp-shooter for that outfit down there. At least he was a week ago…" He thought about it for a second or two and then snapped his fingers. "Wait! There was some kind of accident— something to do with a bear attack. Guess that news was on the money."

He looked at Harry and said, "Okay, I think you need to walk around back and look at those wagons. Could be he's recovering in one of them. That would be pretty easy pickins' right?

It was Harry's turn to frown. "Boss, those Gyps are pretty clannish, you know. They may take exception to me snoopin' around where the women, children and old folks stay hid during their shows."

Tom's natural tendency to having his orders questioned was fury, but he had to stop and think about Harry's observation. He nodded, and allowed, "You're right, Harry. Good thinking… so, yeah, bring the other boys with you. If someone questions why you're not out in the audience, you can just say the three of you got lost. If nothing else, you may be able to spot the kid's location before they boot you out."

Harry nodded, put on his hat and stepped out the door to find his fellow gunfighters, as Tom made his way back to his room to watch the action from above.

———

MANY DARK EYES watched as the three pistoleros slipped through the audience and made their way back into the actual gypsy encampment. Dan watched too, although his eyes were as blue as the sky above. *We figured it right*, he nodded to himself in satisfaction.

It was thought that the men following them would chose the path of least resistance when they set out to find Dan, and that path led from the one hotel in town, down the steps, out into the road, and west into the camp itself. Grandma Nanette's wagon, where Dan hid, was parked at the far, eastern end of camp.

The men were trying to act nonchalant, but their quick, darting eyes and down-turned lips spoke volumes to those that followed them. The gypsies watched as, one by one, the gunslingers stepped aside to check out the wagons. At one point, one of the gypsy's best knife men stepped up to one of their enemies; a small wiry man with close-set brown eyes, and then walked away again, his deadly-sharp knife hidden, as usual, in the sheath under his shirt.

Pedro, who was watching the action from behind a water barrel, grinned with pride. The gunman was in the middle of a huge yawn and scratching his rear-end when his good friend Carlos had gotten up close and personal, but the gunslinger had no clue what had happened

A few minutes later one of the taller gunslingers moved away from his comrades and stepped behind the third wagon down the line but a flurry of offended, feminine shouts filled the air. "You get outta here, you filthy, white bastard!" and, "I will cut your *cajones* off if I see you back here again, *¡gadje estúpido!*" shattered the relative quiet of the campground. Of course, the words the woman used were in Spanish, but their meaning was clear, and the man skipped out from behind the wagon to join his fellows.

It was another fine distraction and Dom Domingo whispered to himself, "Go, Paulie, do it now!" At that precise instant, little Paulie ran up to one of the Pistoleros who stood waiting and stuck something into the barrel of the man's pistol Giving the item a slight twist to secure it in place, he then skipped away out of sight.

None the wiser, the three men strolled along to try and check out the other wagons before they were kicked out of the gypsies actual living area. One of the pistol men, however, a somber, grey-haired fellow with dead eyes, was starting to glare suspiciously, as if he sensed that things were not on the up and up.

And he is right, Domingo thought. *We must finish this quickly or we will lose our edge and make ourselves into targets for these bad men.*

The men passed two more wagons, but these wagons were heavily guarded as they contained all their ammunition, weapons and much of the black-smith's tools-which were still smoking hot from the work he'd done the night before. Many of their toughest men stood close to the wagons and glared at the gunslingers as they passed by.

There were only two wagons to go—an empty

wagon that belonged to Pedro Amaya and Granny Nanette's wagon that housed Daniel and his two deadly pistols. Both the Dom and Pedro held their breath as one of the gunman wandered over to Pedro's wagon and glanced inside.

Happily, the best of all their pickpockets chose that moment to make his move. He stepped up to one of the fattest of the three men and made a clumsy grab at the man's pocket-watch. The fat man started and then let out an angry yell. "Hey, you get back here with that watch!"

But, Jesus kept on running and lost himself in the crowd before the man could let out another frustrated holler. Little did Clancy man know that the theft of his pocket-watch was simply a cover for the real mischief that had been done.

The fat man was still pissed off as hell, though, and making such a racket, the older grey-haired man hustled the other two away from the camp, much to the relief of Dom Domingo, who was afraid Daniel would be forced to open fire when and if he was finally discovered inside Nanette's wagon.

All the gypsies involved stared about and waited for the gun men to come around back again, but a shrill whistle alerted them to the fact that the men had gone back inside the hotel to meet up with that *muy gadje malo* who hid behind the second story window with his long rifle.

Chapter Forty-Nine

ABOUT AN HOUR AND A HALF LATER THE GYPSY FAIR WAS in full swing. Folks from far and wide had heard the news and came in droves to watch the fair, have their fortunes told, check out the new gunslinger, and lay eyes on the tame Cheyenne Indians who were apparently traveling with the show.

The town's population that was, give or take, about 72 souls swelled to five times that much, and the town marshal and his deputy threw their hands up in despair. They knew there was no way they could enforce the law by themselves and all they could do was hope folks behaved themselves the next few days.

Fortunately, the Rom did a pretty good job providing their own security. Nampa's Marshal Earl Tomlin had seen plenty of rowdy customers trussed up and deposited in his own jail over the last few years of the gypsy's circuit, especially if those customers forgot themselves and tried to lay hands on one of their dancers, or refused to pay for services rendered. No one was ever hurt—except, perhaps, for their pride, but it was nice to know that he and his deputy had some silent but willing help today in enforcing the law in Nampa.

Looking around with narrowed eyes, the marshal studied a few men sauntering around in the crowd. There were three or four that stood out, and those men had ridden into town the night before. Tomlin had heard about what happened to old man Burroughs at the town's more reputable saloon the previous evening and he winced in sympathy.

Burroughs had a big mouth sometimes, but he was also the soul of kindness; always willing to give a helping hand to those in need and quite generous with the contents of his coin purse. He gave freely to the new Lutheran church and spent a lot of his money on the less fortunate in town.

It burned Earl up that some hot hand with a gun had shamed Burroughs in front of his peers and he wished he could spot the man and throw his ass in jail. Prudy—one of the town prostitutes—had given him a decent description of the scoundrel. Unfortunately, no matter how hard he looked, that Black feller was nowhere to be seen.

Instead, he found himself gazing at the three men Tom Black had rode in with. One was a little guy with tiny, brown eyes and a gun almost bigger than he was. The other man was as fat as his friend was skinny and carried two big guns on either hip.

Tomlin glared. Nampa was too small of a town to enforce a No-Carry law, but even the stupidest shootist knew that carrying two pistols on his person was as good as wearing a sandwich board that read, **I'm a gunslinger!** over his chest and back.

He almost stepped forward to chase the man down and demand he surrender his guns, but he spied the third man in the group. Earl paused and considered his measly paycheck. He just wasn't paid enough to risk life and limb against a man like that. He was tall and lean but heavily muscled. He had gray hair and cold gray eyes, and of the three men, the marshal knew that one was the worst.

Sighing, he stepped back and searched the crowd for his deputy. *Ah Ha!*, he thought with another disgruntled glare. Davey was standing there watching the knife wheels instead of the crowds, like he'd been ordered to do. Deciding to go grab his wayward deputy, Marshal Tomlin started walking toward the center of the action when gunfire suddenly erupted.

———

DOMINGO AND PEDRO were watching the crowds as well, but with far more anxiety. All the gypsies had skin in this game, and there were a lot of moving parts to contend with. The pistoleros were in play but seemed content with watching out for Daniel, who was even now watching them back through the sights of his guns.

The four men Dom Domingo had assigned to the sniper, Tom Black, had crossed the street a few minutes earlier and stepped inside the hotel. They should be well on their way to subduing that threat, he hoped. Glancing over at one of his oldest friends, he saw the worry in Pedro's eyes.

It had been decided that although some of the younger gypsies had gained some skill in pistol work, none of them were ready or able to contend against professional gunslingers. So, Daniel had to be the one who neutralized the threat, which meant that Emmanuel, Pedro's beloved son, must take Daniel's place on stage—at least, temporarily.

If things worked out the way they planned, Manny would only need to twirl the gun about a bit and wait for Daniel the Two-Shooter to take his place... after Tom Black and his gun men were taken care of, of course.

So, the two men watched as Manny, dressed in new jeans, a snowy white shirt and a rakish black hat bounded onto a small wooden stage, pulled a pistol from his holster and shot it once into the air to gain the crowd's attention.

A few of the customers who'd seen this part of the show before hooted in glee, grabbed their friends and ran over to pay the fee required to watch the young shooter's handiwork. Most of them did not recognize the man-one way or the other. Both young men had raven-black hair and dark eyes. A couple of customers did notice, however, because they had seen Daniel shoot in Kuna, and his height stood out—differing wildly from the diminutive man standing before them now.

Still, the crowd gathered, and held their breath as the youngster stood sideways to take aim at the nearest target. Manny's bullet went left of true center, but nobody noticed because at the same moment he shot his borrowed pistol, a bright red flower blossomed on the boy's chest and he collapsed into a puddle of his own blood as the crowd stood stunned and silent.

Chapter Fifty

THE SILENCE ONLY LASTED A MOMENT THOUGH, BECAUSE suddenly bullets were flying everywhere, and panic set the crowd to running this way and that like a stampede of wild horses.

Pedro and Domingo ran up to where Manny lay groaning on the ground. He was alive, but blood was running freely from the bullet hole in his left shoulder. Pedro, exclaimed, "Oh, my son! I'm am so sorry! This should not have happened... Son! *¡Mi ijo!*"

Manny's large brown eyes had closed, and his olive-colored complexion turned ashy and grey. Dom Domingo bent over swiftly, picked the boy up in his arms and ran toward Granny Nanette's wagon as Pedro followed, hollering for help.

Meanwhile, the four gypsy men who had been ordered to capture and subdue the sniper, Tom Black, had finally finished tying up the wounded deputy, Davey Sniderman, on the second-floor landing. Davey, who had just been soundly rebuked by Marshal Tomlin for goofing off, spied the gypsies making their stealthy way into the hotel, and thought he could get right in his boss' eyes if he were to nab a bunch of gypsy thieves.

His timing was terrible, though, and before the Romany men could stop Black from taking a shot at Daniel the Two-Shooter (who was actually, Manny Amaya) they had to take the deputy down with a knife to the thigh. The young man had cried out in pain when the knife stuck in his left leg, but this was at the same instant that Black shot Manny down.

Looking at one another, and knowing the risk involved in subduing a man with a rifle, they all rushed the door at once. Finding it a flimsy affair, their four bodies entered the room at the same moment Black's rifle boomed. Raphael, a middle-aged man with three daughters took the shot in his face and fell down dead.

Enraged, the remaining gypsy men fell on Black with a flurry of fists, and a poke or two with their knives at the man's less vital organs. Black howled in pain and fury, but within minutes, he was tied up and bound to the hotel bed, being spat on and punched by the infuriated Rom.

———

BLACK'S fellow employees weren't quite sure what was happening, or to whom, but one thing was clear… their orders against using firearms had just flown out the window. Much of the crowd had run away by now, but many of them still lined the street, waiting and watching for what would happen next.

Suddenly, Clarence let out a shout of pain and sagged to the ground as a bullet entered his right knee. He pulled one of his pistols to fire back at his assailant, but for some reason the gun wouldn't budge. Even as his head grew light and his eyes grew dim, he gazed down at his gun and saw that a stout leather string tied the trigger to his gun belt, rendering the pistol useless unless he could undo the knot.

He did manage to untie it, but then his fingers became numb, and he dropped the gun on the ground, and fell next to it in a dead faint.

Seeing Clarence shot galvanized Steve Powell into action. It was clear that this whole affair was turning into a debacle of the worst kind and he had no desire to lose his life over one stupid kid and a gang of unhappy Gyps. Seeing that Clancy was either dead or dying, Steve bent over, grabbed the man's pistol, jammed the extra gun into his gun belt and took off running.

The extra weight was noticeable, but not too bad and he got almost a hundred yards away when his gun belt burst apart and fell to the ground. This was because the belt had been cut almost in half by Carlos two hours earlier. He tripped over the leather and fallen pistols onto his face on the road and, seconds later, four gypsies pounced on him and trussed him up like a prize pig.

Dan nodded his head in satisfaction. That was two down and two to go. This whole scheme had been designed to avoid bloodshed, and Dan was trying his best to keep the casualties to a minimum. A black cloud hung over his heart, though. Manny had been shot, and Dan didn't know whether his friend was dead or alive.

Henry Batre was trying to spot Dan Monroe but having no luck. He was frustrated and angry, figuring by now that this whole scene was a set-up. It was time to cut their losses, but where was Black? He should have a bird's eye view of Dan's whereabouts up in that hotel room, so why wasn't he taking care of things? Unless he too, had been compromised?

Dropping down on all fours, Batre scooted behind a buggy, pulled his pistol and waited for Monroe to show himself.

"Hey, kid! He's over there, behind that black buggy!" he heard a feminine shout. Staring out from behind the spoked wheel, Henry scowled at a red-haired whore who was jumping up and down with excitement and pointing out his location to a tall young man walking slowly his way.

Henry stared in amazement. The kid was limping heavily and holding his gun at his side as if impervious to bullet fire. *Is he crazy?* Henry wondered. *He's gotta know I got him dead to rights...* Henry grinned. *Oh well, whether he's crazy or just plain stupid, don't matter none to me. He's a goner either way!*

Henry stood up and stepped out from behind the buggy as the crowd watched with bated-breath. Dan

Monroe stopped as well, leveled his pistol and gazed back at him with sad eyes.

Henry shook his head and smiled. "Gotta hand it to you, kid. You're as cool as a cucumber." Then, he pointed his revolver, cocked the trigger and fired.

What happened next would be the stuff of tall-tales and legend for years to come. The gypsy's blacksmith had worked throughout the night to fashion a lead plug that would fit the barrel of most pistols currently on the market. It was soft, pliable and grooved on the end, so it would screw into the gun's barrel and stay put.

When Henry casually took aim at Dan Monroe's chest and pulled the trigger, the gun blew up in his hand, effectively amputating his right arm at the wrist. Pieces of sheared off metal blew backward. Henry was blinded and the flesh of his face, neck and chest was mutilated.

Henry Batre fell over backward and died a few minutes later.

Chapter Fifty-One

MARSHAL EARL TOMLIN WAS PISSED AS HELL, AND HIS watery brown eyes stared holes in Dom Domingo and Dan Monroe's faces. Domingo sat impassive, but Dan squirmed in discomfort as the lawman contemplated his story about what had happened two days earlier.

The three remaining gunmen—Tom Black, Clarence Murphy and Steve Powell—were taking up space in Tomlin's jail. They were also singing like canaries. What was surprising, was that the men's stories closely coincided with Dom Domingo and the youngster, Daniel Munroe's tale, although the stories came from differing viewpoints.

Black, and his fellow gunmen claimed that they had been hired to assassinate Dan Monroe by a bad actor named Heck Giddings, who was their long-time boss and the ring leader of a defunct band of outlaws. The bounty on the kid's head was pretty high—$1,500

ALIVE or $1,000 dead. Not a bad pay-off, Tomlin thought with a sour grimace.

Yesterday, he had asked the apparent leader, Tom Black, "So, are you three registered bounty hunters, or was this a private hit?" Earl held his breath—if this was a legally sanctioned bounty hunt there was little if anything he could do about it. That would be up to the U.S. deputy marshals.

Black, knowing his goose was cooked either way, decided to cook Gidding's goose along with his own and answered, "Nah, private business, sir… we was just doing our job."

Tomlin could feel his blood pressure rising and his cheeks turned beet-red at the man's casual shrug. "Your job?' he yelled. "I got two dead men sitting on ice at the doc's office, multiple injuries, including my own deputy and one boy who I hear ain't gonna make it because you were just doin' your job! That's two, maybe three counts of murder, son!"

Black shrugged again, and Tomlin lost his temper. Hauling the injured man to his feet, Earl shoved him down the hall and threw him, none too gently, into the jail cell.

Now, he sat staring at the young pistol-toter, Dan Monroe. He saw a hollow-eyed kid who was only trying to protect himself and his gypsy friends from attack by a powerful enemy. Dan had just got done telling him that he and the gypsies had staged the whole thing to keep the loss of human life at a minimum and Earl couldn't help but be impressed by their efforts.

The kid had done some fine shooting that day, as well. No one he shot at was killed, and Earl had to commend the boy his skill and caution. He smiled slightly and asked, "So, what are you plannin' on doin' now?"

Dan stared at him with surprise and Tomlin saw the boy's tense shoulders suddenly slump with relief. He sat silent for a moment and answered, "Honestly, sir, I just wanna go home. I got some land on the Medicine Bow. Gidding's men burnt my house and barn down but I got enough money to rebuild, I think. I ain't cut-out to be a Pistol Man, sir. Despite I know how, I just want to be a farmer."

Tomlin noticed the old gypsy leader's eyes get big but then saw him nod. Apparently, this was news to him, but Earl felt that Dom Domingo would honor the boy's wishes. He said, "Well, I need you boys to stick around for a couple of weeks until the circuit judge comes to town. You *are* willing to stand as witnesses, right?"

The man and boy nodded, and Earl sent them on their way.

A little while later Earl sat down at his desk and read a couple of local papers. Something about the name Heck Giddings had rung a bell in his head and now, after re-reading a two-month-old newspaper out of Missoula Montana, he realized why Gidding's name seemed so familiar. That crook was paying out favors and bribes, blackmailing and double-dealing left and right to be appointed territorial governor of Wyoming, and apparently about to actually weasel his name onto the President's desk!

Well, he thought, *we shall see about that!*

———

TWO AND A HALF WEEKS LATER, Judge David Koats arrived in Nampa on the train. He was hot and tired, but a grim smile etched his narrow cheeks as he saw Marshal Earl Tomlin and his deputy standing on the front porch of his jailhouse.

Tomlin smiled back and then two big men stepped outside the jail to join the welcome party. Both men sported U.S. Marshall stars and they nodded at the circuit judge with grim confidence. They had been in town for the better part of a week and had gathered all the evidence they needed to put a noose around Heck Gidding's neck.

A few weeks ago, David had given up on being appointed territorial governor, but now he knew that if he still wanted the position, it was his by default. He knew it, the U.S. Marshals Service knew it—hell, even the President of these United States knew it. The only man who didn't know it, yet, was Heck Giddings.

Rubbing his hands together with glee, Koats couldn't wait for that day to come. Especially since he'd discovered that his own son, with Gidding's help, had been trying to sway the nomination toward Giddings by bribing local officials who would recommend the scoundrel to the White House.

He and his son had had words over it a week earlier, and despite his wife's protests, David had cut the purse strings for young Ollie. It was time that boy learned the value of hard work and become his own man—instead of riding on his parent's coat-tails the rest of his life. It was a hard lesson taught and an even harder lesson learned but he was sure that in the long run, young Oliver would become a better man for it.

Koats stepped inside the jailhouse and studied the scum that had taken up residence in this small-town jail. He stood a distance away and refused to exchange words with the men who had come to murder a witness to their boss' crimes, even though they all cried out to him, trying to plead their case.

"I'm innocent, Judge," a skinny man cried out, and, "I didn't shoot nobody, sir!" a heavy-set man with a bandaged knee shouted. The other man in the cell with them remained silent, however. He was better off for it, because Koats knew that this was the man who had started the fight by shooting an innocent gypsy kid named, Emmanuel Amaya.

Koats stepped back from the cell, spat in a nearby spittoon and said, "The trial will start tomorrow at 9:00 am, sharp!"

Chapter Fifty-Two

Seven Months Later

DAN SAT on Jake's grave and read the latest paper from Laramie out-loud, so his pa could hear:

Most Wyoming citizens, at least those who followed the politics of the territorial governor's office, already know what happened on February 28, 1885, in Cheyenne. But for those of you who don't know—this reporter wants to fill you in.

Hector Giddings, who was set to be sworn in as territorial governor, walked into the capitol building that day expecting to receive a telegram from the White House appointing him to the highest office in the territory. I can tell you that the man walked in with a boastful swagger, and he

was surrounded by his equally smug friends and followers.

Instead of giving a victory speech, however, Giddings was placed under arrest by the U.S. Marshal's office for twenty-six counts of murder, bank robbery and train and stagecoach robberies too many to count. He was also accused of attempted assassination and conspiracy to commit fraud. The list goes on but there is only so much space in this Op-Ed, and I have more timely news to report.

Last week, on April 5th, Hector Giddings was hanged by the neck, having been found guilty on all counts by his peers. There was quite a crowd gathered that day, including a representative from President Chester A. Arthur's office and Territorial Governor Francis E. Warren. The majority, though, were folks who wanted to bear witness to the end of a band of bandits who had rained blood and destruction in the Colorado and Wyoming territories for decades.

Still, though the end drew near, Giddings stood with head held high. This reporter thought that the man would hang with not a qualm of guilt, but in the end, he broke down and stared up at the sky as if seeking affirmation from God on high!

The last words he uttered are a mystery to most of those who heard him, including myself, but for posterity, I recorded them faithfully:

He cried out, as if in pain, "Jake! You done for

me, kid. After all I done for you, you still set the hounds of hell on me, and now I'll dance for the devil himself! Damn you, Jake! Maybe I'll meet up with you down there and we can both dance for old Scratch, forever!" Then he fell silent.

When asked if he had anything else to say before he met his maker, Giddings shook his head, and five minutes later, he started his final earthly dance. Now, to the relief of many a citizen, he lies in a pauper's grave two miles away from the sacred ground of Laramie's cemetery.

Now, fellow citizens, we can breathe easier knowing that one of the worst criminals in the western territories has gone on to his reward and will trouble us no more! As we are heading into a new modern century, we the people must unite against evil and revolt against those who would do us harm!

This op-ed has been presented to you by assistant editor-in chief, Raymond Beatty, *Laramie Herald*.

DAN SET the newspaper on the grass and smiled at the ground beneath his feet. "See, Pa? He's done for and won't bother us no more." He frowned a moment, thinking about Heck's final words. Then he added, "and don't you worry none about dancin' for the devil. I know that ain't happening. You're sitting above me in Heaven right now, and smiling down at me, I know it!"

Dan grinned. "Also, Granny Nanette told me so, and I know she knows, fer sure!"

Hearing a shout and a burst of laughter, Dan looked down on the valley below. Two houses had been constructed. They weren't much, yet, but they would be well built and strong given time. One of the houses was his and the other house had been built for Long Knife and his growing family.

Dan had found out, after making his way home, that the Army was standing down on their policy of rounding up all the Indians and were only going after large bands of overtly hostile natives. This was a relief to Dan and to Long Knife, whose family was growing by leaps and bounds.

With the birth of twins, he just wanted to settle down now in peace and security. He also wanted to stay close to his cousin-in-law, Daniel. The boy was becoming a man in his own right, and hardly needed to be looked after, but Long Knife acknowledged—if only in his heart—that he loved the boy and wanted to stay close by his side.

Right now, a bunch of Dan's neighbors had come for a barn raising. Ten men and several women, including two comely young ladies who seemed to be competing for his attention, had come from all around the Medicine Bow to help the young man rebuild. It would take a couple of days, but by Sunday, the pole barn would be standing and ready to house their newly acquired livestock.

Dan and Long Knife had needed to burn about a

dozen skeletons and carcasses when they first arrived and more than once Dan wiped angry tears from his eyes as the flames rose up in the air. Then, a couple of days later, Dan heard a whinny and looking up, saw an old familiar face.

Jonesy was as piebald and ugly as ever, but his big, rubbery lips lifted in a smile as he spied his young master. Dan and the horse ran to each other, stopped in the middle of the clearing and stood nose to nose, breathing each other in.

Speaking of Jonesy, Dan looked over and saw his old companion making its way up the small hill with a rider on his swayed back. "¡*Hola, mi amigo!*" Manny called out with a grin.

Dan smiled back and stood up. "What are you doin riding up here, Manny? You know you're not supposed to ride yet! Granny Nannette will kill me if she hears…"

"But she won't hear, will she, Daniel? Besides the caravan is not due to arrive for a couple of months yet, so don't worry," the young man replied with an impish grin, "Besides, old Jonesy won't let me come to any harm. Isn't that right, boy?" he murmured with a soft smile.

The old horse lifted his upper lip in agreement and tossed its head, as Dan rolled his eyes and sighed.

"Hey, you done talking with your Papá? The women have made a lot of fine food, and I, for one, am starving!" Manny exclaimed.

Dan nodded and said, "You go along, okay? I'm right behind you."

Manny smiled and turned the horse around to head back down the hill. Then Dan placed the newspaper under a large rock that stood for Jake's headstone, and murmured, "I'll just leave this here for you to read, Pa, okay?"

The young man stood up straight then and said, "I'm home for good, sir. Don't worry, I'll never leave you alone again. It's the least I can do for you, who didn't let me stay alone after my folks died."

Dan's throat tightened for a moment, as he knew Jake disliked declarations of affection, but he choked the words out anyway, "I miss you, Pa. And, I'll love you always."

Then he walked down the hill to help with the "barn raising."

A Look At Deadman's Lament

BY LINELL JEPPSEN

The year is 1872. Twelve-year-old Matthew Wilcox leads a charmed life on his family's sprawling ranch in Washington Territory until a series of tragic events leave him orphaned and in the clutches of a vicious band of outlaws. Threatened by the gang leader's perverted cousin, Top Hat, Matthew also faces Indian attacks, dangerous wildlife, and a deadly snowstorm. He survives but burns with an overwhelming hunger for revenge.

Thirteen years later, Matthew - now a Spokane County sheriff - realizes that Top Hat is riding again with a new gang called the Mad Hatters. It means risking his friends, his family and the love of a good woman, but Matthew must find the man who destroyed what he once loved most in the world. To that end, he and his posse venture into Idaho gold country to capture the Mad Hatters.

Top Hat, however, has a different idea. He turns the

tables, heading to the sheriff's hometown of Granville and going after everyone Matthew holds dear.

What follows will haunt Sheriff Wilcox for the rest of his life as he confronts the hatred, vengeance and retribution buried deep in his own soul. Matthew will do anything, though, to put an end to A DEADMAN'S LAMENT.

AVAILABLE NOW FROM LINELL JEPPSEN AND WOLFPACK PUBLISHING

Linell Jeppsen

Linell Jeppsen is a writer of westerns, science fiction and fantasy. Her vampire novel, *Detour to Dusk*, has received over 44- four and five star reviews. Her novel *Story Time*, with over 130 4-and 5-star reviews, is a science fiction post-apocalyptic novel, and has been touted by the Paranormal Romance Guild, Sandy's Blog Spot, Coffee time Romance, Bitten by Books and 64 top reviewers as a five-star read, filled with terror, love, loss, and the indomitable beauty and strength of the human spirit. *Story Time* was also nominated as the best new read of 2011 by the PRG. Her dark fantasy novel, *Onio* (a story about a half-human Sasquatch who falls in love with a human girl), was released in December 2012 and won 3rd place as the best fantasy romance of 2012 by the PRG reviewers guild. Her novel, *The War of Odds*, won the IBD award for fantasy fiction and placed 2nd, as the best YA paranormal book of 2013 by the PRG.